BUMP

MATT WALLACE

 KATHERINE TEGEN BOOKS
An Imprint of HarperCollins Publishers

Katherine Tegen Books is an imprint of HarperCollins Publishers.

Bump

Copyright © 2021 by Matt Wallace

All rights reserved. Printed in the United States of America.

No part of this book may be used or reproduced in any manner whatsoever without written permission except in the case of brief quotations embodied in critical articles and reviews. For information address HarperCollins Children's Books, a division of HarperCollins Publishers, 195 Broadway, New York, NY 10007.

www.harpercollinschildrens.com

ISBN 978-0-06-300798-7

Typography by Andrea Vandergrift

20 21 22 23 24   PC/LSCH   10 9 8 7 6 5 4 3 2 1

❖

First Edition

* * * *

For Arianna, Maya,
Kenny, Maddie, and Abigail

PART ONE:
GREEN GIRL

✶ ✶ ✶ ✶ ✶ ✶ ✶ ✶ ✶ ✶

PROLOGUE: FÉNIX

Everything hurt.

That was what MJ quickly learned about professional wrestling.

It was always hot in Victory Academy, where she had spent most of her after-school hours and weekends for the past month, learning the secrets of pro wrestling. The walls were metal, and after a short while she began to think of the old warehouse like one giant oven in which she was slowly being cooked. The several large fans constantly turning their bladed heads did little to banish the heat. She'd almost gotten used to sweating buckets every day.

MJ stood in one of the wrestling ring's four corners, holding the ropes where they connected to the top turnbuckle. The "ropes" were really steel cables covered by a garden hose slit up its middle and then wrapped in duct tape. MJ still wasn't sure why everyone insisted on calling them ropes. She could barely see over the top of the corner. Even the youngest student in the Academy was almost three years older than her, and she wasn't big for her age besides.

MJ ran in place, her feet pumping as if she were sprinting around the track at school even though she stayed planted in the same spot.

On the cement floor beyond the ropes, Mr. Arellano stalked like some kind of predatory animal in a jungle, circling the ring. The skin around his eyes may've been wrinkled and sagging from age, but those eyes remained clear and sharp, and they seemed to see everything.

"Bump!" he barked at the students inside the ring.

MJ stopped running in place and let go of the ropes-that-weren't-really-ropes. She let herself fall backward, keeping her feet firmly planted where they were on the canvas. She tucked her chin tight against her chest as she landed on the upper part of her back between her shoulders. MJ extended her arms as she fell and slapped her hands against the mat at the same moment her back hit it. She was careful to keep her elbows turned out so they didn't painfully smack the ring floor. It had taken her weeks to master that one small mechanic of taking a bump, and her elbows bore dark bruises that still served as her best reminders.

Landing hurt, just a little, far less than it was supposed to look like it hurt, but far more than people who dismissed wrestling as fake would ever know. Mr. Arellano had told MJ that bumping, especially taking bigger bumps than a simple fall backward, would be harder on her because there was so little padding over her bones, and that it would get easier when she had more meat on her.

It hurt, but it also felt good in a strange way. It sent a rush through her body every time. The truth, as bananas as MJ knew it would sound to most other kids she knew, was that it *all* felt good. The oppressive heat, taking bumps, running drills, bouncing off the ring ropes until the skin under her right arm and across her back wore a red stripe.

After the brief shock of the bump passed, MJ stood up as fast as she could. She grabbed the ropes and began running in place again.

"You need to be back on your feet faster than that!" Mr. Arellano shouted at her from the floor.

Even his yelling at her and the rest of the students all the time felt good. In fact, it was one of the things MJ enjoyed the most. It was the first time in her life that someone yelling didn't make her feel smaller, didn't make her want to shrink away from the source of that yelling and hide. When Mr. Arellano shouted and cursed at them, there was no anger, but there was also nothing held back. He treated his students like adults, even her, and that was the part that felt good.

"Bump!"

MJ planted her feet and let herself fall again, welcoming it, gravity guiding her back to the warm mat that almost seemed to hug her, like a friend.

As she landed, MJ could barely remember her life before the ring, or maybe she just didn't want to.

★ ★ ★ ★ ★ ★ ★ ★ ★ ★ ★

A MONTH EARLIER

Everything hurt.

That was what MJ quickly learned about being twelve years old.

Even if the big hurts were fewer and far between, every day seemed to be filled with little hurts. When the rest of the team had a sleepover and didn't invite you, it hurt. When they friended you on social media just to send you messages that kept you awake at night, it hurt. When a group of older girls shoved you into the lockers as they sprinted down the school hallway, it hurt. When you woke up in the morning and remembered what yesterday was like and you knew today would be more of the same, it hurt.

All those little hurts added up quickly, until they felt

like carrying a big concrete block you couldn't put down.

MJ always kept the blinds in her room shut tight, as tightly as she could pull their rough drawstring. It wasn't that she didn't like light; she didn't like *sunlight*. More than that, she hated the way the world looked in the sunlight, and the way she looked. Sunlight was too bright. It was too *honest*. Everything showed in it, especially imperfections; dirt and dust and stains on furniture, and scratches and bruises and bumps on skin. The fake light from lamps was more forgiving. You could hide things in the soft, muted glow of fake light. Sunlight was like the harsh stare of the kids at her school, always looking for weaknesses in everything and everyone they saw.

So it was dark when she woke up that morning, and she liked it that way.

Her mother felt differently. She marched into MJ's bedroom at 7:01 a.m. just as she did every morning, ignoring MJ stirring in her bed and walking right over to the window, snapping the blinds open and letting the sun invade every corner of the room.

MJ's eyes only shut tighter. She turned away from the light, moaning and pulling her pillow around her head.

"Mom, come on!"

"You keep it too dark in here. It's not healthy."

"The sun gives you cancer, you know."

6

"That's not funny, Maya."

"It's true," she grumbled.

"If you're late again you're going to find out I'm scarier than cancer."

MJ sat up in bed indignantly. "How is that okay, but what I said isn't?"

"Because I'm the mom," her mother insisted.

Still grumbling, MJ crawled out of bed and stumbled across the floor to her dresser. Pulling open the drawer, she fished out a pair of jeans and a baseball-style shirt that had "MJ" printed on the front. Her parents named her Maya Jocelyn. Papi always called her MJ because it reminded him of the character from the Spider-Man comics he read as a kid.

MJ didn't like the old comics much, but she loved her father.

* * * * * * * * * * *

EGGS AGAIN

"**Y**ou have to visit Papi this weekend," her mother reminded her for the third time since Monday.

And for the third time since Monday, MJ pretended not to hear her. Instead, she continued searching the ever-growing mess underneath her bed for the new Vans her mother had bought MJ for back-to-school. After half her body had disappeared into the darkness there, she found the left shoe under a couple of old Ms. Marvel comics.

MJ knew plenty of kids who only visited their fathers on weekends. Maya never thought she would be one of them. She especially didn't think it would be like this.

She tried. Every day she tried, but she couldn't stop being mad at her father for leaving, even in the quiet moments when she really, truly *wanted* to not feel that anger any-more, when she just wanted to miss him being there for her, just wanted to be sad about what was happening. That she actually wanted to be sad and couldn't be just ended up making her even angrier, however.

"I know you hear me, Maya *Jocelyn*," her mother repeated, adding MJ's middle name in that way parents had probably been doing since the first time a parent yelled at their child.

"I hear you," MJ grumbled, snatching her right shoe from behind a Corrina Que Rico action figure grappling with a Stevie Lord action figure (she liked to have her Corrina beat up on the guy wrestlers).

"Everyone understands what you're going through," her mother said, more gently. "Papi understands, too. I didn't want to make you visit him until you were ready, but if you keep on like this, you'll never be ready, and that's not going to work, Maya. This is the way things are now. I've tried to give you time to get used to it on your own, but I have to start helping you do it. That's my job. Your job is to try, okay?"

"I *am* trying," MJ insisted. "I'm like the captain of the Get-Used-to-New-Stuff Team practically."

Her mother sighed. MJ hated that sound. It was like a horn her mother blew every time MJ let her down.

"I know, baby. Get your shoes and your schoolbag and come to the kitchen, okay?"

Her mother left her bedroom. MJ waited until she heard cabinets opening and dishes rattling in the kitchen before she finally crawled out from underneath the bed. She folded her legs in front of her and put on her shoes. The carpet felt stiff and unfamiliar beneath her. It was brand new, like everything else in the small house they were renting. One of the reasons the room was such a mess was because MJ had just dumped out the few boxes she'd brought with them from their old house when they'd moved in four months ago, and then shoved the contents of each box under the bed.

MJ slipped the phone from her front pocket. She unlocked it and tapped the little talk bubble icon. Sure enough, Papi's last voicemail was waiting for her. She didn't listen to it. She also didn't delete it. MJ hadn't been able to bring herself to do either.

"Come eat your eggs!" her mother called.

MJ cringed. Almost every morning since Papi left them her mother had made MJ huevos rancheros for breakfast. It was the only dish her mother knew how to make, and she was terrible at it. Papi always did the cooking.

She put away her phone and forced herself to stand up. Her backpack, notebook, tablet, and schoolbooks were spread across the tangled sheets and blankets of her bed. MJ stuffed them into the backpack and zipped it up before running out of the room.

MJ's mother called the kitchen a *kitchenette* because it wasn't its own room like in their old house. It was narrow and separated from the living room by an ugly copper bar top. MJ sat at the little round table where they ate all their meals.

There were a bunch of papers scattered on the other side of the table. Her mother had been going over their bills last night after she sent MJ to bed. Before MJ fell asleep, she could hear her mother worrying out loud, sighing and muttering to herself.

She wouldn't talk to her daughter about it, but MJ knew they didn't have a lot of money, or at least they didn't have as much as they used to. That's why they were renting this small house, and why her mother had to sell the old one they'd lived in all of MJ's life.

Because of that mess of papers on the table, and what the papers meant, it seemed like all her mother did these days was work, way more than she had before. When they were in their old house, before Papi left, they'd spent almost every weekend visiting with her father's family. They'd barely seen any of the family since they'd moved, and hadn't even moved that far. Her mother was too busy, although MJ sometimes wondered if Mom liked having that as an excuse.

Her mother put a glass of milk and a plate of huevos rancheros atop a tortilla in front of her. MJ tried very hard not to make a face as the smell hit her nose. The eggs smelled like hot ketchup and they looked like brains heaped onto a plastic frisbee. Papi made his own tortillas from scratch. Abuelita had taught him how. Her mother bought the ones from the store that felt like rubber in your mouth and tasted like wet cardboard.

MJ poked at the red mess with her fork as her mother sat down next to her with a cup of coffee.

"Are you not hungry?" her mother asked.

"I don't want to be late," MJ lied.

"Oh, really? What's happening at school today?"

She shrugged.

Her mother frowned at MJ over the rim of her coffee mug.

"When are gymnastics tryouts?"

It was MJ's turn to frown. "It doesn't matter, 'cuz I'm not going out this year. I told you."

"You said you'd think about it, as I recall."

"Oh. Well. I meant I'm not going out this year."

"Maybe I can come to school with you and take a class in this new language you've been speaking lately."

"Ha-ha," MJ shot back at her.

"Why don't you want to do gymnastics anymore? You were getting so good at it."

"I don't like the kids."

"What's wrong with the kids?"

"They're kids."

"And what are you?"

"Something else. At least that's how they treat me."

Her mother was quiet for a while.

"Why didn't you tell me last year that was happening?" she finally asked MJ.

She shrugged again. "There was a lot going on."

"Yeah, I guess there was. I'm sorry, Maya. Maybe we can—"

"Can I go now?"

Her mother treated her to another sigh, then said, "Take three good bites, then you can go."

"How about one really big bite?"

"Stop negotiating with me and eat," her mother ordered her.

MJ took a deep breath and quickly shoveled three fork-fuls into her mouth, chasing each bite with a big gulp of milk to wash out the taste.

"Do you want something different tomorrow?" her mother asked her as MJ got up from the table.

MJ shouldered her backpack. "How about money to go to McDonald's?"

"I hate you so much," her mother said with a wicked grin, shaking her head.

"Hate you too, bye!" MJ called back to her cheerfully as she ran toward the front door.

CHICAS MALAS

Lunch was both her favorite and her least favorite period of the school day.

She liked it because she could be alone, and usually no one bothered her. She didn't like it because sometimes she got tired of being alone, and during lunch there was nothing going on to make the time pass faster like there was during class.

Even though she and her mother had moved, MJ was still attending the same school. Mom said it was because it was the best in the district, and she wasn't going to let MJ go to a school that wasn't as good. MJ could tell it meant a lot to her mother, keeping her here. Selling their old house had been really hard, and MJ knew her mother blamed herself.

That's why MJ had such a hard time being mad about moving, or at least being mad at her mother. She could see how much pain it caused Mom, and MJ didn't want to add to that. Besides, as much as she loved their old house, after Papi left, every room reminded her of them all being together, and that always hurt.

Going to a different school was one change MJ wouldn't have minded making, though. The kids at her school always seemed so stuck up to MJ. And most of them didn't look like her. She never really talked about that, not even to Papi, but she noticed. She noticed every day.

MJ bought chocolate milk from one of the school's vending machines. There was a spot behind the library where MJ liked to sit against the wall and watch wrestling on her tablet while she ate her lunch.

Lucha Dominion was MJ's favorite pro-wrestling show, and they put out a new episode every week. She had their app loaded onto her tablet so she could keep up with it and watch extra stuff like interviews and behind-the-scenes videos. Unlike other wrestling shows, which ran all year long every year, Lucha Dominion happened in seasons like a regular TV show.

"So this is where you hide now?"

MJ looked up in alarm.

It was Madison. She was the top-ranked gymnast their

age in the state and one of the worst people on the planet, or at least that's what MJ thought.

Madison was flanked by Emma and Sophia, the other stars of their school's gymnastics team. The two of them weren't so bad, except when they were around Madison, and then they were like hyper puppies someone kept poking with a stick. It wasn't hard to understand why. Not only was Madison their team's undisputed leader, her dad was their gymnastics coach. No one wanted to cross her.

Besides, MJ thought, the three of them *looked* like they belonged together. They all matched. They were like an advertisement for The Pretty White Girl Store.

MJ had managed to avoid them since the school year started three weeks ago, but her luck had finally run out.

"I'm just eating my lunch," MJ said, returning her attention to her tablet, hoping they'd go away.

None of them moved.

"We didn't see you at tryouts," Madison said.

"That's because I wasn't there. I'm not doing gymnastics anymore."

Madison folded her arms across her chest and smirked. "Why not?"

MJ didn't answer her, because telling them the truth would just make Madison say even meaner things, and probably do worse than that.

"I hope you don't think you're too good for us, or something."

MJ still didn't answer.

The truth was they'd been so mean to her that even the thought of showing up for gymnastics practice made her want to cry.

Her silence and the way she was ignoring them made Madison angry.

"Look at me when I'm talking to you!"

MJ sighed. She paused her Lucha Dominion video and slowly raised her chin, staring up at the three of them.

Madison's expression was like something out of a comic book panel. She looked like a Marvel villain who'd just been beaten up by Wolverine or something.

"Are you still watching that junk?" she asked, nodding at the frozen image on MJ's screen.

Madison had always liked making fun of her wrestling obsession, but MJ was used to people doing that.

It only hurt now because wrestling was one of the things she shared with her papi.

"Obviously," MJ said, too quietly to even be heard through her grinding teeth.

"I told you what my dad said about people who watch wrestling, right? How they can barely be smart enough to tie their shoes?"

MJ blinked hard as if she'd just been stung by a bee. The mention of Madison's father hurt even worse than any of her insults. She remembered all too well the way their coach felt about wrestling. He'd always barked at her to "turn that junk off" whenever he caught her watching her tablet before practice.

"I didn't try out this year because I just don't want to do gymnastics anymore, that's all."

Madison glared at her.

MJ waited, her heart beating faster. She felt like she was sweating, and she hoped they couldn't see it.

"You are so pathetic," Madison said after a while.

There was so much hatred in her voice. MJ couldn't understand why.

Madison kicked over the plastic bottle of chocolate milk sitting opened on the ground beside her. MJ had to scoot away to avoid the milk that spilled across the cement. She reached down and picked up the bottle while there was still some left inside.

Madison watched her and laughed. The other girls didn't laugh. They just stood there with nervous smiles on their faces. She wished they'd say something, but she knew they were too scared of Madison and her dad to ever do it.

Fortunately, they walked away after that.

It wasn't what they did to her that really bothered MJ,

it was that she had to take it. That was the part that made her feel so powerless and angry. She wanted to fight back, but she didn't know how.

MJ drank the sip of chocolate milk that was left in the bottle, and then she unpaused the video she was watching.

Listening to Corrina made her feel better.

Wrestling was still there for her, even if Papi wasn't, and it helped her deal with the real world.

It didn't fix things, but it helped.

SHIPWRECK

MJ would never have guessed that losing a drone over a wall one day could change her life, but it did.

It was the last present her papi had given her before he left them. It was red and black and looked like a helicopter from the future, and she could control it with an app on her phone that he'd shown her how to use.

MJ liked it because she didn't have to go outside to play with the drone. She could sit in her bedroom and control it from the window, sending it dive-bombing at soda cans she'd set up in their new backyard.

She hadn't felt like arranging any new targets that day, so instead MJ aimlessly guided the drone in zigzagging patterns inches above the dying grass. A six-foot concrete wall separated their yard from the house next door. The top of it always seemed to have seeds and pods from a nearby tree scattered over its rough surface.

MJ navigated the drone above the wall and carefully let it settle close to the top without quite touching. Gently edging it forward so its round body tilted, MJ revved up the speed and let it fly. The force created by the drone sent dried yellow pods shooting out from under it on both sides, clearing the top of the wall. It was satisfying to watch, and MJ felt proud of herself and her little electronic pet.

That satisfaction turned to sudden panic when the front of her drone snagged against a particularly rough spot in the concrete and went flipping end over end beyond the fence, disappearing into the neighbor's backyard.

"Uh-oh," she breathed quietly to herself.

MJ couldn't see where it landed. She tried to summon it back into the air with the controls of her phone app, but the drone wouldn't rise. It was either stuck on something, or the crash had damaged it.

MJ felt that bubbling begin in her gut that happened when she knew she was about to be in trouble.

She put her phone down on the windowsill and pushed herself up by the edges of her seat, unfolding her legs and hopping down from the chair. MJ bolted out of the house as fast as she could run, charging across their backyard to the place at the wall where her drone went down.

She realized she had no idea who lived here; in the four months since they'd moved into the house, she and her mother hadn't really met anyone on the street yet. MJ had only seen an aging truck parked in the driveway next to theirs from time to time, but it hadn't been there when she'd come home from school, so she was pretty sure nobody was home.

Standing next to it, the wall seemed a lot taller than it had when she looked down at it from her bedroom window. MJ licked her lips nervously, thinking she should just wait until that truck pulled back into the neighbor's driveway and then she could go knock on the door and ask for her drone back. Then she thought about what would happen if the neighbors didn't come home before her mother did. She could just not tell Mom about the drone, of course, but what if the neighbors found it and brought it over? Then not only did MJ crash the expensive gift, she would also have lied about it.

And it was a gift from Papi; not just a gift, but his last gift to her.

Running through every possibility like that made her head hurt. MJ shook her head to clear away those thoughts, telling herself that she was acting like a dork, and that she *wanted* her drone back.

She bent at her knees and launched herself into the air, reaching up and gripping the top of the wall. The unfinished concrete dug into her fingertips, but she was easily able to pull herself up and swing her legs over.

It actually felt good to move her body like that. MJ wouldn't tell her mother, but she missed gymnastics. MJ missed the way she felt free when she flew across the practice mats or walked the balance beam. It was everything that happened when she stepped off the mat that she couldn't stand.

She dropped down into the neighbor's backyard, landing solidly on her feet. The backyard hadn't been mowed in weeks, it seemed, and the grass was up to her ankles.

Still, she spotted her crashed drone lying next to an old, cracked marble fountain with a sculpture of Our Lady of Guadalupe on top of it. MJ recognized the image of Mary from her abuelita's candles. She sprinted over and picked up the drone, examining it for damage. The plastic body was chipped where it had snagged the rough concrete, but other than that MJ couldn't see anything that would prevent it from flying. She hoped its inside parts weren't messed up too bad.

MJ looked up from the drone and really took in the yard for the first time. Other than the disused fountain, there was only one other thing on the overgrown grass, but that thing dominated most of the space. She wasn't sure how she hadn't noticed it when she first hopped the fence.

Something giant was covered by a dirty canvas tarp in the corner of the yard. Whatever it was, it was twice as tall as MJ and the size of two minivans. MJ crept toward it, curious. At first she thought it might be a project, maybe some old boat somebody was working on restoring on the weekends. Then MJ noticed the tarp was split down one corner, revealing a piece of what was hiding underneath.

The object poking out was a tall, rusted metal post.

MJ squinted at the long rectangle. There were ropes or cables connected to two sides of it, and under those, hanging from the edge of some kind of platform, large pieces of cloth draped down to the ground.

Her eyes widened as she recognized what she was looking at.

She walked over to the exposed corner of the tarp and touched the metal post carefully. It was rough on her hand, but it seemed solid, like it wouldn't easily tip over.

MJ hesitated, biting her lower lip. She knew she shouldn't be there, let alone doing what she was thinking about doing.

She bent down and placed her drone back in the grass. MJ reached out and grabbed two handfuls of the canvas tarp. She gave them a tug. The tarp barely moved. Taking a deep breath, she dug her heels into the ground beneath the tall grass and pulled as hard as she could. Slowly, the tarp began to slide over the top of the object. MJ had to turn around and drag the end of the tarp she was holding over her shoulder. The rest of it finally pulled away and after trudging over a dozen steps MJ felt the bulk of the tarp drop to the ground.

She let go of the piece she was holding and turned back to take in what the tarp had been covering up.

It was a wrestling ring, just like the ones she'd seen on TV all her life. It certainly wasn't as impressive as those, nowhere near as polished and clean. In fact, this ring looked to be in terrible shape. The "ropes" looked to be wrapped in duct tape that was several different colors. The canvas covering the inside of the ring was dirty and torn in many places, several of which were also patched over with duct tape. The turnbuckles that connected the ropes in each corner, which were usually covered by pads, were mostly just exposed, rusted metal rings.

MJ didn't care, however. She'd never been this close to a real wrestling ring before, and she thought it was amazing.

It's not yours, a voice that sounded a lot like Mom's said inside her head. *This isn't your yard. You shouldn't be messing around with other people's stuff.*

All of that was true, but how often would MJ be alone

with a real-life pro-wrestling ring?

Besides, how could she be in more trouble than she already was?

She crawled underneath the bottom rope and across the stained, taped-over canvas, standing up in the middle of the ring. It didn't feel the way she thought a ring floor would feel under her feet. Her family members who thought pro wrestling was dumb always compared it to a trampoline. It didn't feel like that at all. The ring floor felt solid underneath the layer of canvas on top of it.

MJ gently rocked back and forth from the tips of her shoes to her heels. There definitely *was* some give to the ring, though. She gently bounced up and down several times. It felt like jumping on wooden boards with nothing underneath them. She didn't think it would feel good to fall on this floor, however.

"¡Oye!"

It was a deep, angry voice, and as it hit her ears MJ jumped and felt her blood rush and go cold.

She looked over her shoulder. An old man in a black suit and tie was standing at the back door of her neighbor's house. She hadn't heard the truck pull into the driveway, but this had to be its owner.

He reminded her of pictures MJ had seen of her grandfather, though she'd never met the man, who passed away long before she was born. The deep lines in this old man's face and his steel-gray hair, perfectly combed back, were exactly like that image of her abuelita's husband. Her new neighbor looked much tougher, though, without the kind smile her grandfather always displayed in those old pictures.

"What the hell do you think you're doing in there?" he demanded, sounding angrier with every word. "I should call the cops right now!"

MJ couldn't force words from her brain to her mouth. That only made her panic more. Without thinking, she looked away and ran to the corner of the ring nearest to the fence, quickly climbing up the turnbuckles. She balanced herself easily on the top rope and gingerly leaped from the ring to the top of the fence.

"Get down from there!" He continued to yell angrily at her. "Hey, I'm talking to you, girl! Come here! Come here, I said!"

He was still raging loudly as MJ dropped over the fence into her own yard and ran into the house, slamming the back door behind her.

* * * * * * * * * * *

SEÑOR ARELLANO

That evening they ordered pizza for dinner and MJ tried to say as little to her mother as possible. Fortunately, ever since they'd moved, MJ's mom was used to her daughter not saying much during dinner, or really any other time they were together.

It was almost eight o'clock and MJ was sitting on the living room floor in front of the couch, scrolling through YouTube clips without actually watching anything. Her mother was in the kitchen rinsing and putting into the dishwasher the few dishes they'd used. MJ was starting to think that maybe she was in the clear, at least for the rest of the night.

The knock at their front door sent MJ's heart leaping

up into her throat. Her first impulse was to run to her room and close the door, but she knew that was pointless. At a loss for anything else to do, she pulled in her arms and legs and tried to make herself as small as possible against the front of the couch. She felt stupid, knowing she couldn't turn herself invisible no matter how much she wanted to, but she tried all the same.

Her mother came out from behind the kitchen bar and walked across the living room. After checking through the peephole to see who had knocked, she unlocked and opened their front door.

It was the old man. He was holding her broken drone in hands that looked as though they'd been through a war a long time ago. They were scarred and withered, though somehow, they didn't look weak. He'd changed out of his suit and tie and was now wearing gray slacks and a black polo shirt with a logo on the breast.

Peeking over the couch, MJ noticed the logo right away, even in her panicked state. It was a large red luchador mask, with a *V* sewn to the left of it and an *A* sewn to the right of it.

The old man was smiling. He didn't look mad anymore, which made MJ feel better, but she was still terrified of what was about to happen and how Mom was going to react.

"Buenas tardes, señora," he greeted MJ's mother. "Mi

nombre es Álvaro Arellano. Soy su vecino—"

"I'm very sorry," her mother interrupted him, smiling uncomfortably. "I don't speak Spanish."

MJ knew that was always a sore spot for her mother, especially with Papi's family, who were all from Mexico and whose native language was Spanish. MJ's grandpa, Mom's father, was a white man from the Valley, where her mother was born. Even though he'd married MJ's grandma, who was from Tecate, and even though MJ's mother was half Mexican and looked like it, they didn't speak Spanish in their house when MJ's mother was a little girl. It always seemed like it embarrassed her mom when people spoke Spanish around her, especially when they assumed she did, too.

"Oh. Excuse me. My name is Álvaro Arellano. I'm your neighbor."

Her mother seemed relieved, not only that the old man spoke English, but that she had a new subject to talk about instead.

"Oh! Hello! It's very nice to meet you. We've been meaning to introduce ourselves around the neighborhood. I'm Vivian Medina, and this is my daughter, Maya."

"I believe your daughter and I met earlier today. She was in my backyard."

"Oh?" Her mother looked back at MJ and frowned. "I'm so sorry. I didn't know that happened."

"No, no," Señor Arellano said quickly. "I guess she lost one of her toys over the fence, and she was just trying to get it back. Actually, I . . . I think I owe her an apology."

Her mother's frown only deepened.

"Maya!" she called to MJ. "Get over here!"

MJ swallowed, setting aside her tablet and standing up slowly. She walked around the couch with her head down and her eyes on the floor, not looking up until she was standing beside her mother.

"Hello, Maya," Mr. Arellano said.

She tried to smile. "Hi."

He took a deep breath. "Listen. When I met you this afternoon, I . . . I had just returned from Mexico. And I'm sorry to say I wasn't in a very good mood. You see, I was there for . . . for a funeral."

Her mother's frown softened, as did her eyes. "I'm very sorry to hear that, Mr. Arellano."

He nodded. "Gracias. Thank you."

"May I ask who passed?"

Mr. Arellano dropped his head for a moment. When he raised his eyes to meet Vivian's, it looked as though he'd been blinking back tears.

"My grandson," he said quietly. "He was fifteen."

MJ watched her mother's hands cover her heart.

32

"I am . . . *so* sorry."

MJ felt her own stomach twist into several knots. For a moment she wasn't afraid of being punished anymore, she just felt a deep wave of sadness to hear that someone not much older than her had died.

Mr. Arellano cleared his throat.

"Anyway. I wanted to apologize for yelling at you like that, Maya, and I wanted to return this."

He held out her drone.

MJ didn't do anything at first. She couldn't stop thinking about what he'd just told them about his grandson.

"Maya," her mother nudged her. "Take your helicopter. Say, 'Thank you.'"

"It's not a helicopter," MJ grumbled, low enough that no one said anything.

She reached up and took the drone. "Thank you."

Mr. Arellano smiled, still looking sad, and nodded to her.

"I'm sorry I was in your ring. I just . . . I've never been in a real wrestling ring before."

"Maya loves the TV wrestling," her mother added, although she sounded confused at the mention of the ring.

MJ frowned. She hated it when Mom called it "TV wrestling."

"I understand," Mr. Arellano said. "Don't worry about it. I was just afraid you might hurt yourself. That thing is such an old piece of junk."

"Why do you have a wrestling ring in your yard?" MJ asked.

"It's the ring I learned to wrestle in."

MJ's eyes lit up.

"You're a wrestler? A real wrestler?"

"A long time ago, mija. A *very* long time ago. Now I teach. I have a school in the old Santa Fe District."

"That's very interesting," MJ's mother said in a way that made it clear to both of them she didn't know what else to say.

MJ knew her mother did not find wrestling interesting.

"Well, I don't want to disturb your night anymore," Mr. Arellano concluded. "I just wanted to introduce myself, say sorry, and give back your not-a-helicopter."

He winked at her with a grin after saying the last part, and MJ laughed without thinking.

She stopped when she realized her mother was looking at her strangely. It might have been because MJ couldn't remember the last time she'd laughed like that.

Mr. Arellano turned to leave their doorstep.

"Could I go to your school to learn to wrestle?" MJ asked quickly, again acting without thinking.

"Maya!" her mother reprimanded her.

MJ blinked up at her innocently. "What?"

It was Mr. Arellano's turn to smile uncomfortably. "It's not as easy as it looks on TV, mija."

"I don't think it looks easy," she insisted.

"How old are you?"

"I just turned twelve."

"You're too young. And a little on the scrawny side, if you don't mind my saying."

MJ frowned. "Do you not train girls?"

"Maya *Jocelyn*!" her mother snapped at her. "You are being so rude right now!"

"No, no," Mr. Arellano reassured her. "It's fine, señora."

"Vivian, please."

"Vivian." He looked back at MJ. "I've trained dozens and dozens of luchadoras. My niece is Corrina Que Rico."

"No way! I love her! She's my favorite!"

Mr. Arellano nodded. "We're all very proud of her. But she started out at my school. She still comes to train when she's home."

"Then why couldn't I train at your school, too?"

"First of all," her mother interjected, and the way she said each word felt to MJ like a punch. "You didn't ask *me*, young lady, and you know very well there is no way I would ever let you do something like that. And even if that weren't true, he just told you, you're too young and you're too small."

"I am not!" MJ fired back before she could stop herself.

Her mother's eyes flashed what looked to MJ like fire, and she knew she'd crossed a line.

"Your mother is right, mija," Mr. Arellano assured her, breaking the tense silence. "You should listen to her."

MJ wanted to say that no, her mother *wasn't* right, but MJ knew she was already in enough trouble.

"Thank you for stopping by, Mr. Arellano," her mother said politely. "Have a good night."

"You too. Nice meeting both of you."

He walked away from their front porch and MJ's mother shut and bolted the door behind him.

MJ didn't move. She stared down at the carpet, which she thought was the ugliest brown color she'd ever seen, and bit her lower lip.

She could feel her mother's eyes burning into her.

"So then," she said while taking a deep, cleansing breath. "Before I ground you for the rest of your natural life, do you want to tell me about you being in this ring thing?"

MJ knew that at this point in the conversation what she wanted didn't really matter anymore, but she also knew better than to say that.

★ ★ ★ ★ ★ ★ ★ ★ ★ ★

THE WALL

Third period always smelled like cough syrup.

It had taken MJ a few weeks after she started sixth grade to figure out why. Their homeroom teacher, Mrs. Sanchez, liked to pop a cough drop in her mouth before each new group of kids shuffled in. MJ caught her pulling one out of a bag in her desk and unwrapping it one day when she'd walked into class early. When the mean-looking woman opened the drawer, it was like a bomb went off that made the room smell like a hospital.

She still wasn't used to it. There were a lot of new things about sixth grade she was trying to get used to. The middle school was new, and although a lot of kids she'd known or seen in fifth grade were there, it all felt strange and scary to her. It didn't help that MJ hadn't had any close friends before her entire grade had all moved up from elementary school.

Once a week they had a free period in Mrs. Sanchez's class, during which they weren't required to do anything. MJ still didn't understand why, but it was a thing. She had heard other kids talk about using their tablets or listening to music during free period, but Mrs. Sanchez didn't allow any of that because she hated anything that made kids happy, or at least MJ thought so. Mostly, the kids in her class just sat and talked quietly. MJ had never been much of a talker at school, so she usually just spaced out the whole time, letting her mind drift away until she stopped noticing where she was.

That day MJ was thinking about Mr. Arellano and his wrestling school. It was pretty much all she thought about since meeting the old man. MJ just *had* to figure out a way to get him to let her come to his school, even if only to see what it looked like and what happened there.

She was working on formulating a plan when she heard a voice behind her say, "Lucha Dominion."

Surprised, MJ glanced over her shoulder and saw a group of three girls huddled together. They were speaking quietly, but MJ heard enough to understand they were talking about Corrina Que Rico, and Corrina's big upcoming match on the season finale of Lucha Dominion with her nemesis, Avispa Vudú.

MJ didn't know two of the girls talking about MJ's favorite show, but the third was Sophia. She was one of Madison's closer friends from the gymnastics squad, but Madison wasn't in Mrs. Sanchez's class with them.

Sophia noticed MJ looking in their direction, and the only reason MJ didn't look away was shock.

What was even more surprising was that Sophia smiled at her.

You should say something, MJ thought. *She was your friend, too. Wasn't she?*

It had always felt that way, at least. She'd gotten along better with Sophia than she ever had with any other kids.

Madison was the reason they all shut her out. Madison didn't like people she decided were outsiders, and she'd decided on their first day sharing a gym mat two years ago that's what MJ was. The only thing Madison seemed to like less than outsiders was her friends hanging out with, or even being nice to them.

That might have been why Madison still came after her so hard. The other girls had liked MJ. It didn't matter that she didn't talk much, or that she was a little awkward. MJ was nice, and more importantly, at least on a gymnastics team, she was *good*. The other girls had been impressed by her skills. That only angered Madison more and made her work even harder to push MJ away and make sure the other girls did the same.

MJ had taken it for as long as she could, but without Papi around to make her feel better, she knew she couldn't last another year on the team. He'd never known how bad it was for MJ, because she was too afraid to tell him, but when she did talk to her father after a hard practice it still made her feel better.

Even thinking about trying to deal with everything happening at home *and* Madison at the same time was too much.

But Madison wasn't in their free period. Sophia wasn't under her influence right now; she seemed friendly, and they were all talking about MJ's favorite thing in the world. It was the perfect opportunity to do something.

MJ opened her mouth, but nothing came out. She knew what she wanted to say to them. In her mind she could see and hear herself speaking clearly and with confidence, but she just couldn't make her thoughts reach her lips. It was like hitting a wall and bouncing off it. That wall was always there, between her and anyone outside of her family, it seemed.

In the end, MJ frowned and looked away from the trio

of girls without saying a word, though she called herself all sorts of names in her head.

Behind her, MJ heard Sophia's friends giggling and whispering about what a weirdo MJ was.

She didn't hear them *say* that, but that's what it sounded like in her head.

Madison would be happy, MJ thought. She'd won again, and she wasn't even there.

* * * * * * * * * * * *

CORAZÓN

MJ decided that 7:00 a.m. was the earliest she could stop by Mr. Arellano's house without being a pest and still make it to school on time, and she was waiting on his front step right on the dot. She'd barely slept the night before, thinking about what she wanted to say to him and how she was going to say it. She also knew her mother would be furious if she knew what MJ was about to do.

Somehow, it didn't matter to MJ if she was punished further for being here. For the first time since Papi left them, she really wanted something. In fact, the more she thought about it, MJ could only think of one thing she'd ever wanted as much as she wanted this, and that other thing wasn't going to come to pass.

This she could get, if she tried hard enough and was convincing.

At least, MJ hoped that was true.

She knocked on Mr. Arellano's door and waited. In her hand MJ held her tablet. Her thumb was ready to scroll through several Wikipedia pages she'd saved on the device's internet browser.

The door creaked open slowly and the old man stood there in a ratty old red and black bathrobe. His eyes were bleary, like he just woke up, and the hair that had been perfectly combed back every time she'd seen him so far was now sticking out in several different directions.

"I hope you're selling something," the old man told her without taking the time to say hello.

"Cookies, maybe?" he asked. "I like cookies."

MJ frowned. She decided in that moment that if he wasn't going to waste any time then she wouldn't either.

Instead of explaining why she was there, MJ launched into the important part of the speech she'd planned late the night before.

"Rey Mysterio Junior wrestled his first match in Mexico when we was fourteen years old!" she proclaimed, holding up her tablet displaying Mysterio's Wikipedia page as proof. "That means he started training even earlier than that. It doesn't say when on Wikipedia, but he had to be my age, and maybe even younger!"

Mr. Arellano's bushy gray eyebrows wrinkled up as he looked down at her in confusion.

"What are you talking about, girl?"

MJ took a deep breath and went on, ignoring the question. "William Regal was only fifteen and he was wrestling people in carnivals for real. The Apache sisters were seventeen and eighteen when they had their first matches. Riho started training when she was *nine years old*, and I'm already as tall as her!"

"What's your point?" Mr. Arellano demanded.

She felt that rising in her chest—the cold rush in her blood that caused shivers. It was the feeling of doing something that scares you.

"You said I'm too young and too little to train to wrestle. But . . . you're wrong. If Rey Mysterio Junior could wrestle in his first match when he was only a couple of years older than me, why can't I start training now?"

"You're comparing yourself to probably the most famous luchador since Mil Máscaras?"

"He wasn't always the greatest. When he started he was just a little kid like me, and he wasn't any bigger, either. I'm practically as big as he is *now*."

Mr. Arellano actually laughed at that.

MJ started to smile, but the old man suddenly stopped

laughing. He didn't look annoyed anymore. He looked sad, like he'd just had a thought that bothered him deeply.

"Rey Mysterio and the Apache sisters all come from lucha families," he said. "They grew up with it. They were practically born to be workers. It's something that was passed down from their fathers, and their father's fathers."

"Just because they came from a family of wrestlers doesn't mean they were better than anybody else when they first started."

He sighed. "I guess that's true, but I'm sorry, Maya, you should concentrate on school. *Real* school."

"I'm sorry if I made you sad."

Mr. Arellano looked confused. "What do you mean?"

"I'm sorry if asking you to train me makes you think about your grandson. I didn't come here to make you sad."

He frowned. "That has nothing to do with this."

MJ wasn't sure she should say anymore, but she'd come too far to chicken out now.

She decided if telling him the truth didn't convince him, then nothing would.

"I know . . . I know how it feels when people leave you. I know how it feels when things change. It sucks. I just . . . I *love* wrestling. And I don't . . . there's nothing else I love right now. There's nothing else that makes me feel the way wrestling makes me feel. It's the only thing that makes me happy. And that's just watching it."

Mr. Arellano stared down at her silently for what felt like a long time. His eyes looked cloudy, like the beginning of a storm.

Finally, he said, "Whenever my life turns to crap . . . perdóname . . . whenever things go bad or wrong in my life, I always turn to the business. It's the one thing that's always there."

"The business?"

"That's what we call wrestling. What you're asking me to do is break you into the business."

"Will you?" MJ asked hopefully. "Break me into the business? Please?"

Again, he was quiet for a while before answering. MJ could tell he was thinking hard about this.

"¿Hablas español?"

MJ understood he was asking her if she spoke Spanish.

"A little," she said

"Entonces contéstame en español," he pressed her.

MJ had to concentrate, pulling the words from the back of her brain.

"Hablo un poco. My grandma . . . mi abuela me enseñó."

Mr. Arellano nodded.

"You'll learn to speak lucha."

MJ took a deep breath and held it. "Does that mean I can come to your school?"

"It was brave of you to come here like this. It shows you have heart. Heart's the most important thing in this business. It's not muscles or good looks or being a great athlete. This business is hard. If you don't have it in your heart, it'll kill you. Do you understand?"

MJ nodded.

"What about your mother?"

"I'll talk to her," she insisted. "I'll tell her how much it means to me. She'll let me do it, I swear."

"You're a minor. You have to get your parents' permission and they have to sign a waiver for you in case you get hurt. That means I'm not responsible. And you're going to get hurt. If you listen to me it won't be so bad, but this isn't acting, whatever your friends at school or your parents or whoever thinks about wrestling. I've had over a dozen concussions and I've broken almost every bone in my body in the ring."

"I understand," MJ said, trying to sound as serious as she could.

Mr. Arellano nodded, looking satisfied.

"Bueno. I'll pick you up Saturday morning, nine o'clock, *if* you get your mother's permission, which I doubt."

MJ felt like she was going to bust apart from the excitement she felt.

Then she thought of something else.

"Oh, I should have asked, how much does it cost? To take lessons from you?"

Mr. Arellano took a long, deep breath. He looked like he was deciding something.

"I'm not going to take your money," he said. "At least not until you try it and decide whether you want to come back."

MJ couldn't imagine why she wouldn't want to come back, but she didn't say so.

"What's it called? Your school?"

"Victory Academy," he said with pride in his voice.

★ ★ ★ ★ ★ ★ ★ ★ ★ ★ ★ ★

THE DEAL

"**N**o."

"You said you wanted me to join a team. This is the same thing!"

"No."

"I can use *all* of my gymnastics!"

"No."

"It'll only be after school and on weekends!"

"No."

"I'll meet new people and make new friends!"

"No."

"Please!"

"No!"

It was their third conversation about it that day. MJ felt

like she was making progress. When she'd first brought up the idea of her mother letting her attend Victory Academy, she shut MJ down in less than a minute. The second time MJ raised the issue, her mother yelled at her for about five minutes before telling MJ to stop asking her. This time, however, they'd been going back and forth on the subject for almost ten minutes, and her mother had only just raised her voice.

They were sitting on the couch in their living room, and her mother was trying to watch some dumb show that MJ hated.

She hadn't watched a show she actually liked on their television since they moved. MJ and her mother just didn't share the same taste in things like movies, music, and TV shows. Papi was the one who had watched what MJ liked.

"Mom, will you just think about it?"

Her mother paused the show for the fourth time since she'd started watching it.

"Maya, I have thought about it. The answer is no."

"You said no as soon as I asked! That's not thinking about it!"

"I'm the mom. I don't have to form a committee before I make a decision."

"This is important, though!"

"You *just* found out this school existed like, two days ago!"

"I've loved wrestling my whole life!"

"Being a fan of it is fine for a kid. Being a wrestler is ridiculous."

MJ fell quiet. Hearing her mother say that hurt her feelings more than she would've thought. Judging wrestling so harshly was a lot different than trying to keep MJ from doing something that was potentially dangerous, or at least it felt that way.

The expression on her mother's face softened a little when she saw how her words had affected her daughter.

"Look, maybe we can revisit this when you're a few years older, okay?"

"Who knows if I'll even have this chance when I'm older, though? What if Mr. Arellano stops teaching by then? It's not like there's a wrestling school on every corner or anything."

"Then you won't be a wrestler, I guess, and I'm sure you'll find something else to do with your life."

"How can I know if I want to do it or don't want to do it if I never even try?"

"Maya, I'm sorry, but the answer is still no."

Her mother unpaused the show, and the two of them

sat in silence for several minutes.

MJ's head was spinning. Part of her brain was telling her to stop pressing the issue and not to push her mother any further, but a much louder part of her brain told her if she gave up on this now, she would never get another chance like this.

She couldn't let it go. She just couldn't.

"Mom?"

Her mother grunted in annoyance and paused the show once again.

"What is it now?"

"I'll go visit Papi."

Her mother looked at her in surprise.

"What?"

"Let me go to *one* class at Victory Academy," MJ said carefully, "and I'll go visit him."

To her surprise, her mother didn't get mad. Instead, she looked genuinely distressed.

"Maya, that is . . . *so* unfair."

MJ knew what her mother meant, and she felt bad for having said it. All her mother had wanted since they moved was for MJ to stop being angry with her father for leaving them and go visit him. It *was* unfair of MJ to use that to try and make a deal with her.

She wasn't willing to take it back, though. MJ wanted

to train at Mr. Arellano's school too much.

"I'm sorry," she said. "I know it's not fair. You're right. I don't . . . I'm not trying to be a bad person. I just feel like . . . like I need this right now, you know? Nothing else helps. I hate school. I don't want to be around other kids. Talking to the family only makes me feel even worse. Even talking to you, and I know how hard you're trying to help. I really do. It's not your fault. But meeting Mr. Arellano and hearing about Victory Academy . . . it's the first thing I've wanted that isn't wanting Papi to come back. It makes me feel better. Is that wrong?"

She was really asking, because MJ didn't know.

Her mother could see that. She could tell by the way she was looking at MJ in that moment.

"No, it's not wrong," her mother finally said. "It's not wrong to want to feel better, or to have something that takes your mind off things. I'm just worried this is a bad way to do it, that's all. They hit people with chairs and smash them through tables and all of that."

"Mom, no one's going to hit me with a chair. It's training. It's like practice. I'll probably just learn the really basic stuff."

Her mother groaned, covering her face with her hands, and MJ knew that meant she was considering it now.

MJ stayed quiet. She thought saying any more might

hurt her chances instead of helping.

After a while her mother stood up from the couch without saying anything. She left the living room, walking down the hallway toward her bedroom.

When she returned, she was holding a small notebook and a pen. She sat back down and began to write.

"What are you doing?" MJ asked.

"This piece of paper is going to be two things," her mother explained. "The first thing is a set of rules you have to follow if you're going to do this. The second thing is a contract. When I'm done you're going to sign it. That means you're promising me in *writing* that you're going to follow these rules and abide by them and their consequences. Understand?"

"What are the rules?"

"First, this isn't going to affect school. *At all.* Do you hear me, Maya? If you miss any school because of this, or especially if your grades start to drop, you're done. No discussion. Okay?"

MJ nodded.

"Second, if you come home hurt, you're done."

MJ frowned. "Well, what does 'hurt' mean? How hurt is hurt?"

"Anymore hurt than you'd get doing gymnastics."

"Kids break stuff doing gymnastics all the time!

Stephanie got a concussion last year when she fell off the balance beam!"

"And she was out for the rest of the year!"

"I could get hurt doing any sport, Mom."

"I don't care! If you break a bone, or hurt your head doing this, it's over! Do you understand?"

"Fine," MJ relented, grumbling. "Bumps and bruises?"

Her mother sighed. "Bumps and bruises are fine. I guess."

"Okay. But . . . I can go, then?"

"We'll *try* it. Okay? One class. Just to see what it's all about."

MJ could barely contain her excitement. She threw her arms around her mother's neck and kissed her on the cheek.

"Thank you so much!"

Her mother hugged her with one arm, patting her between the shoulders.

"It is nice to see you happy about something again, I will say that."

"I am. I am really happy. Thank you, Mom. I mean it. I know this is a big deal. I'm taking it seriously."

"I can see that. And Maya?"

"Yeah."

Her mother reached up and gently took MJ's chin in her hand, gazing into her eyes softly.

"You don't have to go visit Papi until you're ready, okay? I'm not making that part of the contract."

MJ nodded, not knowing what to say to that, but she did feel relieved.

Her mother finished writing out the rules. The last thing she did was draw a line underneath what she'd written, marking the line with an *X*.

She presented the notepad and pen to MJ.

"Sign there, please."

MJ took the pen and wrote her name in careful cursive on the line her mother had drawn.

"Good," her mother proclaimed. "This is binding. Don't make me haul your little butt into court."

MJ grinned at her.

Her mother sighed, tearing the piece of paper out of the notepad and carefully folding it into several halves. She tucked it into her pocket.

"I must be the worst mother in the world," she said.

"You probably are, yeah," MJ agreed, nodding in an overly solemn way.

In response, her mother tackled her onto the couch, struggling to pin her arms down. MJ tried to fight her off while they both laughed.

"I better take advantage before you learn what you're doing!" Her mother fake-growled.

They eventually ended up rolling onto the floor, where they continued to wrestle and laugh until they were both out of breath.

Lying there, huffing and smiling and staring at the ceiling with her mother beside her, MJ felt lighter than she had in a long time.

THE ROPES

Saturday morning, MJ stood outside of her house feeling a little sick to her stomach. It was weird, she thought, that she'd fought so hard with both Mr. Arellano and her mother to be given this chance, and now as she waited for the old man, she was suddenly scared of what was about to happen. MJ supposed she'd been so wrapped up in convincing them to let her try that she hadn't actually thought about what would happen if they both said yes.

She realized that she had no idea what to expect or what going to a wrestling school meant. Mr. Arellano had only told her wrestlers get hurt. She was smart enough to know that watching wrestlers on a screen didn't mean she was ready to be one.

What if she wasn't tough enough? What if she wasn't smart enough to learn? What if they were both right about her being too young and too small and she got hurt? What if she embarrassed herself in front of Mr. Arellano's other students?

MJ almost wanted to turn around and run back inside the house, but her desire to see this through was greater than her fear. Besides, she couldn't back out, not after what she'd gone through and put her mother through to make it this far.

Mr. Arellano picked her up in his old truck as he promised. MJ was ready for him. She'd dressed in tennis shoes, yoga pants, and an athletic top she hadn't worn since gymnastics season ended the previous year. She was also holding the forms he had given her, all of them signed by MJ's mother.

They didn't talk much during the drive. MJ was filled with questions, but she was afraid that asking them would reveal how scared she was.

The only question he'd asked her was, "Did you eat breakfast?"

MJ told him she'd just had a banana and some juice.

"That's good. Your body needs fuel, but you don't want to eat anything heavy before you train, especially the first time."

She didn't know what that meant, and the thought of finding out only made her more anxious.

The school was a large converted warehouse downtown. There was nothing remarkable about the outside of the old building except for two things: a small painted sign that displayed the school's logo and the words *Victory Academy* spray-painted in red letters across the outside wall that faced the street.

Mr. Arellano told MJ the warehouse was once a dress factory, and that women who looked like her mother had been paid pennies to work twenty hours a day there. He also told her that was one of the reasons he had bought the building years ago. He wanted to use it to help their people achieve the dreams their parents were never given the chance to pursue. MJ wasn't sure she knew exactly what Mr. Arellano meant, but she knew her grandparents had worked very hard at backbreaking jobs to give her mother and father the education and opportunities in life they had not been given.

Victory Academy on a Saturday morning was a beehive of activity. There were dozens of people training inside the warehouse. There was a collection of soda and snack vending machines against the wall with some tables and chairs in front of them, which seemed to be where everyone in

the Academy took their breaks between classes and social-
ized. The school had a gym area set up in one corner with
weights and exercise equipment, and all of it was being well
used by the students.

A lot of them, even in their exercise clothes, looked
the way MJ expected professional wrestlers to look, either
attractive and athletic or hulking and menacing. However,
many of the students seemed just like regular people to MJ.
Seeing those students training made her feel better, less nervous about being there. It even made her start to believe she
could really do this.

The Academy had three different wrestling rings. Two
of them were smaller and lower to the ground than the
ones MJ had always seen on TV, and they looked only a
little bit newer and cleaner than the one in Mr. Arellano's
backyard. The third ring, however, was big and impressive
and looked a lot like the ones MJ's favorite wrestlers bat-
tled inside on the shows she watched. It was set up in the
middle of the warehouse, and high above it, stage lights
were hung from a metal rack attached to the ceiling. There
was a lot of empty space around that third ring, too. MJ
wondered if that space was left open to set up chairs so they
could hold wrestling shows at the school.

MJ also noticed there was a thick red line painted on

the cement floor a few feet away from the wall; it seemed to circle the entire warehouse. She couldn't imagine what that was for.

"Wow," she said, in awe as she looked around for the first time.

"It's not much, but it's home," Mr. Arellano told her.

"I think it's great."

"What's up, Papi!" someone called from the other side of the warehouse.

It felt like suddenly walking into a brick wall, hearing the name MJ called her father yelled out like that. It stopped MJ cold and made her body tense up. She looked at Mr. Arellano as he waved casually to the student who had shouted to him.

It was the first of many such greetings he received from the students in the school. MJ soon realized that everyone at the Academy called Mr. Arellano *Papi*. It was obviously a name they used out of affection and respect for him as their elder and their teacher.

"Oye, Papi!"

A young Mexican man with long, stringy hair jogged up to them with a big smile on his face. He was wearing gym shorts and a torn T-shirt along with old-looking knee and elbow pads, but his boots were tall and patent leather, like the ones many of the wrestlers on TV wore. MJ wondered if he was a professional rather than a new student.

Mr. Arellano hugged the younger man and patted him on the back.

"Welcome home, mijo," he said.

When they stepped apart, Mr. Arellano turned to MJ.

"Maya, this is my nephew, Hernán."

"What's up, girlie?" Hernán warmly greeted her. "Call me Creepshow."

"Is Creepshow your wrestling name?"

His face took on a wounded expression. "You mean you never heard of me?"

MJ felt trapped suddenly. She didn't know what to say.

Creepshow quickly dropped the expression and laughed. "I'm just messing with you."

"Oh," MJ said, relaxing.

"Hernán works in Japan, mostly," Papi explained. "He just got back from a sixteen-week tour with RealTime Combat, one of the big wrestling companies over there."

MJ was impressed. "Wow, really? Japan? Is it cool?"

"Best crowds outside of Mexico," he assured her.

"Can I look you up on YouTube?"

"Yeah, but you might not recognize me," he warned her.

"They like gimmicks based on horror movies over there," Mr. Arellano explained, "so they put him under an ugly Halloween mask. That's why they call him Creepshow."

"That's really cool," MJ said.

"I need to talk to this tipo for a minute," Mr. Arellano told MJ. "Wait here."

She nodded, and then watched as the two of them walked away. There was an area in the back of the warehouse that was separated from the rest of the space by tall black curtains. In the center of them, an archway had been erected. It looked like it had been cobbled together from rough pieces of scrap metal. A spray-painted sign reading VAWF was hung above it.

Mr. Arellano (*Papi*, MJ reminded herself) and Creepshow soon disappeared through the folds of black cloth beyond that archway. Those curtains certainly backed up her suspicions about the school also being used to put on real wrestling shows.

She felt awkward being left alone. MJ shifted uncomfortably from one foot to the other, wishing she weren't by herself, while at the same time scared to talk to anyone new.

MJ distracted herself from her jangling nerves by watching what looked like a class taking place in one of the smaller rings. Half a dozen students were lined up against one side of the ring ropes. They each took turns rolling forward across the ring before popping back up to their feet.

One of the girls in the ring actually looked as though she wasn't that much older than MJ. She made MJ think of the kids one or two grades ahead of her at school. The girl stood at least six inches taller than MJ and seemed even taller with the gorgeous pile of curly hair atop her head. She had long arms and legs, and MJ thought she looked really cool in her black singlet and matching knee and elbow pads. She reminded MJ of Serena Williams.

It took a second or two for MJ to realize the girl was staring back at her. When she did, MJ's cheeks suddenly felt like they were burning. MJ knew she should look away, but instead she just blinked.

Instead of looking down at her from the ring as if she thought MJ was some kind of weird creeper, the girl just grinned and giggled. She waved down at MJ.

It took a few seconds, but MJ finally managed to wave back. She even felt her lips beginning to smile.

"Maya, come over here!" Mr. Arellano called to her.

He was standing at the edge of a collection of old gym mats spread out atop the concrete floor. He wasn't alone. A young woman, maybe eighteen or nineteen years old, was standing next to him. She had a smile on her face and her curly hair was dyed three different shades of fiery red and orange. She wore a black and pink wrestling singlet with leggings that extended all the way down into her black workout boots. The laces of the boots were also bright pink, to match her singlet. MJ saw there was a bandana tied around the upper part of her left arm, an arm that also had several tattoos.

MJ quickly sprinted over to the gym mats to join them. Her eyes were on the older girl.

"This is Tika Powers," Mr. Arellano introduced her. "She's one of our top students and biggest draws here at the Academy. She just turned pro a few months ago. Tika, this is Maya."

"Hey!" Tika greeted her, waving enthusiastically as if MJ was far away and not standing right in front of her.

"She's going to get you started training," Mr. Arellano said.

MJ looked down at the mats on the bare floor.

"Here?" she asked.

"You start out here, on these mats, learning to wrestle," Mr. Arellano told her seriously. "Not flying around, or throwing chairs and ladders, or doing any of that crazy stuff you see on TV. You start with *wrestling*. And you don't get to put a foot in a real ring until Tika says you're ready. Understand?"

MJ nodded.

"Speak up, girl," he instructed her. "You didn't have a problem doing that when you came to my door at sunrise."

"I understand," she said, adding quickly, "Papi."

The old man nodded. "Good. I'll leave y'all to it."

He walked away without another word.

"Don't let him scare you," Tika said after he was gone.

"You can call me MJ. Everybody does except my mom."

"Okay, MJ."

"Is Tika your wrestling name?"

"My gimmick name, yeah. But that's what everybody calls me, too."

Tika stepped onto the mats and motioned for MJ to follow her.

"You ready to do this?" she asked.

MJ took a deep breath. "I'm nervous."

Tika's smile only seemed to grow bigger and brighter. "I feel you. I was too. I was terrified my first day here. And you know what? I *sucked*."

MJ couldn't help but laugh at that.

"I did!" Tika assured her. "I tripped over my own dumb feet for the first like, six months. It takes a long time before you start to get good, and I just mean getting good at doing drills and taking bumps and stuff. Working an actual match is a totally different thing. So don't worry, okay?"

MJ nodded, trying to make her brain accept what Tika was telling her.

Tika turned slightly sideways and spread her feet out so that they were in line with her shoulders.

"All right, stand like this," she instructed MJ.

67

MJ tried to copy what the older girl was doing.

"That's really good," Tika said, and she sounded as though she meant it. "I can already tell you pick things up quick."

"I don't know about that," MJ muttered.

She grabbed MJ's wrist and placed MJ's hand on the top of Tika's right shoulder. Then Tika put her own hand on MJ's left shoulder.

"Now, put your other hand on top of my bicep, just above my elbow," Tika instructed her.

MJ did as she was told, and then watched as Tika again mirrored her.

"This is locking up. It's also called a collar-and-elbow tie-up. This is how you start the match ninety-nine percent of the time."

MJ nodded. "I know. I've watched wrestling pretty much my whole life."

"Good. Now, you'll see a lot of people grab the back of the neck, but I always do the shoulder."

She squeezed MJ's shoulder gently for emphasis.

"From here, like you see in almost every match, you can go just about anywhere. We're going to work on chain wrestling first, okay? I'll show you all the basic holds, and all the counters for them."

MJ felt a thrill rise through her body. She thought she'd be eager to start body-slamming people and jumping off the ropes as soon as she set foot inside Victory Academy, but in that moment she couldn't think of anything more exciting than learning these seemingly simple holds from a real wrestler like Tika.

After Tika took MJ through all the basic holds and reversals, they spent an hour practicing them. MJ lost count of how many times they locked up. Tika showed her how to both apply wrist- and head- and hammerlocks and how to make it look like being in those holds was causing MJ great pain. She showed MJ how stringing together a long combination of holds and reversals could create an exciting sequence to watch, as entertaining as any high-flying or big power move.

"All right," Tika said when they stepped apart for the last time. "I think you're ready to take some bumps."

MJ remembered her saying that word before, but she still wasn't exactly sure what it meant.

"Bumps?" she asked.

"Falling down and learning how to land. Taking big bumps for your opponent is pretty much all you're going to do when you first start working matches."

MJ's eyes lit up. "Oh, right!"

She led MJ to one of the empty smaller rings and hopped up onto the edge of the platform just outside the ropes, an area MJ had heard called the "apron." MJ watched as Tika carefully rubbed the bottoms of her boots against the canvas before stepping through the ropes.

"Remember to wipe your feet," Tika told her.

MJ climbed up after her and did exactly what she'd just watched Tika do.

Tika stepped to the middle of the ring and motioned for MJ to join her.

"We'll start with a basic back bump."

MJ nodded eagerly.

"Bend your knees," Tika told her, demonstrating. "The key thing is keep your feet planted, even when you land. Don't move your feet. Watch."

Tika fell back with practiced ease and grace. It wasn't a big sound when her back hit the canvas, but the impact made MJ blink and jump just a little. She also noticed that as Tika landed, she threw her arms to the side and slapped the canvas with the flat of her hands.

She looked up at MJ from the ring floor. The bump didn't even seem to have rattled Tika.

"Now, see how I landed, on the upper part of my back? And I kept my chin tucked so I don't hit the back of my head on the mat. The last thing to remember is to slap out."

To illustrate, Tika spread her arms and slapped the canvas again with both hands.

"Got it?" she asked.

"I . . . think so."

Tika popped up to her feet with speed and a grace that made MJ jealous.

"Okay, go for it," she said.

MJ stood the way she'd watched Tika stand, bending her knees. She took a deep breath and then let her body fall back, remembering to keep her chin tucked and her feet planted squarely in place like Tika instructed her to do. The top of her back hit the mat, or at least that's where MJ felt the bump the most. More than any kind of pain was the shock she felt run through her whole body.

"Good!" Tika complimented her. "But remember to slap out."

"Oh, yeah," MJ said.

She slapped her hands against the mat.

Tika laughed. "You have to do it as you land. It helps break the bump. You don't have to do it after. Okay?"

MJ felt her cheeks flush red. "Right. Got it."

"Now, don't sit up. When you take a back bump like that, remember to turn to your right and push yourself up, okay? That's how your opponent will pick you up off the mat."

MJ nodded, crossing one leg over the other and rolling onto her stomach before pushing her body off the mat and standing up.

Tika had her take several more back bumps, and by her fifth or sixth MJ barely had to think about slapping out at the end. After that, Tika showed her how to front bump, falling forward onto her stomach. Those, MJ found, took even more wind out of her than falling onto her back, but she was able to pick up the proper form and technique quickly.

The final bump Tika showed MJ was falling onto her side, taking most of the impact on her hip. That one was the most awkward for MJ. It felt way less natural than the other two ways of bumping, and Tika said they'd have to work on that one more later.

"Don't worry about it," Tika said when she saw MJ looking discouraged. "Everybody has trouble with side bumps at first."

Hearing that helped, at least a little.

"You feel okay?" Tika asked her.

"Oh yeah," MJ answered excitedly. "I feel great."

"Yeah, that's the adrenaline," Tika warned. "You're going to feel a lot different tomorrow, believe me."

"It's worth it," MJ insisted.

Tika grinned. "I like you."

MJ looked at her shoes. "Thanks a lot."

"You feel like running the ropes?"

She looked up, beaming. "Totally!"

Tika nodded. "Okay. The ropes will bite you if you're not careful. I know they feel like rubber on top, but underneath is a steel cable."

"So they're not really ropes?"

"Sometimes they are. The big companies use rings with real ropes. But here we train on the cables, and you gotta learn how to hit them right or they can really mess you up."

MJ crinkled up her nose in confusion. "Why would I hit the ropes?"

Tika giggled, just a little. "You don't really hit them. It just means when you bounce off them."

"Oh, right, like when your opponent whips you into the ropes."

"Exactly. Now, *this* is where you should make contact with the top rope."

Tika lifted her arm and rubbed the muscle just below her armpit.

"You want to wrap your arm around the top rope as you hit it. That's so in case the rope breaks you'll already be holding onto it and you won't go flying out of the ring."

"I understand," MJ said.

"Good. The other important thing to remember is to just use your natural momentum. Don't throw your body against the ropes. Just kind of turn and let them take your weight and push it off on their own. And keep your feet planted flat when you hit them. Don't rock back on your heels. I'll show you."

Tika demonstrated by running into the ropes several times. MJ watched a different part of Tika's body each time it bounced against them, trying to memorize what she did with her feet, then her arms, then her torso.

When it was MJ's turn to try, she checked off a list in her head of all the things Tika had just told her and demonstrated. She planted her feet and shook out her arms and her legs for a few seconds, then started running across the ring. The first few steps felt good and natural, but when it came time to turn her body and bounce against the ropes, MJ froze up without even meaning to. She only managed a half-turn, and it felt more like she crashed into the ropes than let her body fall into them.

Tika was right about them biting her, too. She felt the sting against her back.

"It's okay," Tika assured her as MJ regained her footing. "You just hesitated. Try it again. Clear your head and don't think about it so much. Just let your body do the work."

MJ closed her eyes and tried to let her mind go blank. She took a few more deep breaths. As soon as she opened her eyes, she took off running, and this time she didn't freeze. She just rotated her body and let herself go. Gravity and the spring in the cables did the rest. Gravity flung her into the ropes. The ropes accepted her weight and bounced her back across the mat. MJ ran with the momentum before coming to stop right beside Tika.

"That was great!" Tika shouted. "You kept your feet flat and everything!"

MJ could feel the smile spread across her face. It felt good, even better than taking the bumps. Bouncing off those ropes made her feel free, like being fired from a giant sling shot and flying through the air, only she was running.

"Try it again," Tika urged her.

MJ did. She ran the ropes, from one side of the ring to the other, over and over again until she was out of breath and felt like she'd sprinted a mile. By the end of it the muscle under MJ's arm was throbbing and sore. She lifted her arm. She could already see the bruise welling up along the strip of her skin that had made contact with the top rope.

"You'll get used to it," Tika promised her. "You'll get

used to all of it. Don't worry."

"Who's the green girl?" a new voice asked from somewhere outside the ring.

MJ recognized that voice immediately. She'd heard it on her tablet and her phone almost every week for the past two years.

She looked over and saw Corrina Que Rico standing at the edge of the ring apron on the other side of the ropes. She wasn't wearing her wrestling gimmick, of course. She was dressed in regular street clothes, jeans and a Lucha Dominion hoodie.

"Hey, Cory," Tika greeted her as if Corrina Que Rico wasn't a famous luchadora on national TV.

"Hey, girl," Corrina said back to her cheerfully.

It sounded like they were friends. Tika immediately became even cooler in MJ's eyes.

"This is MJ," Tika explained. "I'm breaking her in. First day."

"How old are you?" Corrina asked MJ.

"Twelve."

Corrina looked puzzled. "No manches! Are you a cousin I don't know about, or something?

"Um. No?"

"Papi doesn't usually train kids unless they're family."

"I, um, sorta talked him into it, I guess."

Corrina made an impressed sound. "Then you already know more about the business than me, chica. I can't talk that old man into nada."

Getting such a huge compliment from one of her heroines, MJ couldn't help but smile, though she didn't know what to say to that.

Fortunately, Corrina didn't wait for her to respond. "Well, you got a good teacher. Tika is going to be signed before you know it."

"Don't play," Tika chastised her.

"Who's playing? Don't think I don't know you're gunning for me."

Tika waved the entire subject off with a shake of her head.

Corrina looked back at MJ. "I'm gonna leave you to it. Good luck, mija, okay?"

"Thank you," MJ all but squeaked.

Corrina walked away. MJ desperately wanted to say something like, "You're my favorite!" Or even, "I love you!"

Instead, she just watched silently as one of her wrestling idols crossed the gym.

"What does 'green girl' mean?" MJ asked Tika when she was sure Corrina couldn't hear them anymore.

"'Green' just means you're new in the business, that's all."

"Oh."

MJ was quiet for a moment, and then she asked, "What color are you, Tika?"

Tika laughed long and hard at that.

* * * * * * * * * * *

ZINA

It was a week after her first training session at Victory Academy when MJ found out the purpose of the red line painted around the school.

She was bent over, hands holding her knees, and breathing so hard she was worried she might throw up. She had just run around the school, inside that painted line, a full ten times. Mr. Arellano told her doing that meant she'd run a mile.

"Breathe in through your nose and out through your mouth," he said, watching her. "Like I told you before. That's how you keep from blowing up when you're in the ring."

"Blow up how?" MJ managed to ask through panting breaths.

"Blowing up," he repeated. "Getting tired and running out of breath. Getting blown up is as bad as getting hurt during a match. It stops you from doing anything. You have to learn how to breathe and pace yourself."

"Yes, Papi," MJ said, trying to draw air in through her nose and release it from her mouth.

After a few seconds of doing that, MJ found that she could breathe more easily. The rest of her sweating, aching body began to relax, too.

"That's better," Mr. Arellano said, sounding pleased with the way she took his instructions.

"Stand up straight," he told her.

MJ did, pushing off her knees and straightening her back.

"Go get a Gatorade out of the machines and take a break."

MJ nodded, walking past him toward the common area with all the tables and chairs.

"Gatorade," Mr. Arellano repeated. "Not soda."

"Si, Papi!" she shouted back to him.

As MJ approached the vending machines, she saw a familiar face. It was the girl MJ had watched doing drills in the ring when she first walked into Victory Academy, the tall black girl who smiled and waved at her. She was sitting on top of a table with her booted feet on one of the chairs, drinking from a bottle of water. She was alone, too, just scrolling through something on her phone.

MJ really wanted to talk to her.

She thought about the girls on the gymnastics team, and how they treated her. MJ didn't want that to happen here.

She already loved coming to Victory Academy. She didn't want to ruin it. She decided not to say anything.

Then the older girl looked up from her phone for a second, but before she returned her attention to the screen, she smiled at MJ.

Something about her smile made MJ rethink her decision. Instead of walking past her and going to the vending machine, MJ stopped in front of the girl.

"Hey," she managed to force past her lips.

"What's up?" the older girl said, still smiling.

Okay, that went well, she told herself. *Now act like a normal person and tell her your name.*

"My name's Maya. Most people call me MJ."

The other girl smiled wider. "Like from Spider-Man?"

MJ blinked, surprised. "Yeah. Exactly."

"Did you see *Into the Spider-Verse?*"

Not only had MJ seen it, she loved that movie.

"Oh my god, it's so good!"

"Right? So good!"

MJ felt herself relaxing, like when she was at home.

"I'm Zina," the older girl said.

"That's a cool name. How long have you been training?"

Zina shrugged. "A few months. You just started, right?"

MJ nodded.

"I thought I was the youngest one here. What grade are you?"

"Sixth. You?"

"I just started high school."

"Wow."

"Yeah, it's . . . different."

"Good different or bad different?"

Zina seemed to think about it.

"I don't know yet. You know?"

"I think so. Do you do other sports?"

"Not really. I played basketball and softball when I was little, but the older I got the less I liked it. I don't really do good on teams, you know?"

MJ's eyes lit up a little bit. "Me either! Even when I was really little, I always wanted to do individual sports."

Zina nodded wisely. "You definitely find a lot of individuals in this gym."

MJ smiled more easily than she had in a while. "I guess so. How did you get into wrestling?"

"My brother. He's a wrestler. He trained here with Papi."

"Really? What's his name?"

"Daniel, but his gimmick name is Stroke."

MJ thought about it, but she couldn't remember a wrestler named Stroke.

"You might not know him," Zina said. "He's never been on TV or anything. He's an indie guy."

"Indie?"

"Independent. Like, not part of a big company on TV or anything."

"Oh, right. Okay. That's really cool, though. I never knew anyone who was a wrestler before I met Papi."

"Well, you know plenty now."

MJ nodded. "Yeah, for sure."

It occurred to her that this was the longest and best conversation she'd had with another girl even close to her age in a long time, and maybe ever.

"I was really scared after my first class that my mom wouldn't let me come back," MJ said. "But I guess seeing that I didn't come home with any broken bones was enough to convince her to let me keep coming, for now anyway."

"It's a lot for folks who don't know the business, I guess. So you're feeling it so far? Training here?"

MJ nodded again, but faster and more enthusiastically this time.

"I love it here."

Zina grinned. "Yeah, me too. I think it's made for people like us who don't do so good on teams."

MJ thought about that. Victory Academy seemed very much like a family, but everyone she'd met here did their own thing. That seemed to be what professional wrestlers were: a bunch of people performing individually to create something together.

"That's pretty cool," MJ said. "I hadn't thought of it like that."

Zina nodded, but didn't say anything else.

MJ wasn't sure what to say next, either. That was usually when she would've run away from the exchange, scared by the silence and afraid of embarrassing herself.

Instead, she said, "I was gonna get a Gatorade. You want one?"

Zina finished the rest of her water. As MJ watched, she crushed the bottle down into a small lump, and then twisted the cap on so air wouldn't blow the bottle back up like a balloon. She tossed the crumpled bottle at the nearest trash can, and it landed perfectly inside.

"Sure," she said, grinning.

Zina was about the coolest girl MJ had ever met.

* * * * * * * * * * *

RUDO

MJ and Mr. Arellano were talking about their favorite wrestlers as he drove her to Victory Academy. He was telling her all about legends like Blue Demon and El Santo, who were the most famous luchadores in Mexico when he was a boy.

"They weren't just wrestlers," he told her. "They were like movie stars and superheroes all mixed up together."

"Like if Spider-Man was a wrestler?"

"I suppose so."

"I read online that Stevie Lord is going to be in a movie."

"I'm sure that will be a masterpiece," Papi said sarcastically.

"You don't like Stevie Lord?"

"He's not bad for a gabacho."

"He's one of the biggest stars on Lucha Dominion!"

"Like I said, he's not bad for a gabacho."

"What was your gimmick name?"

Mr. Arellano smiled with pride. "I was El Hacha Rojo."

MJ squinted in thought, trying to place one of the unfamiliar Spanish words.

"The red . . . what?" she asked.

He laughed. "Axe, mija. The Red Axe."

"Oh. Were you famous when you still wrestled?"

"I wasn't Santo or Blue Demon, that's for sure."

"But you were a big star in Mexico?"

"My son was bigger," he said, and somehow he sounded proud and sad at the same time. "He was better than me, too."

"Where is he? Does he still wrestle?"

"He passed away, mija."

"I'm really sorry, Papi," she said, and for some reason, after hearing about what happened to his son, it was easier for her to call him that.

"It's okay. It was years ago."

"How did it happen? Is that okay to ask?"

"What happened to him happened to a lot of workers from his generation. On the road too much and for too long, wrestling too many shows. He started taking medicine for the pain from his injuries. And he took other things because he missed being away from home, and because he was spending so much time in strange cities and in hotel rooms. One night he took too much of both those things, and when he went to sleep he didn't wake up."

"That's so awful."

"I took care of his son after because his mother wasn't able to. My grandson had the same fire and the same talent. He would've been as great as his papi. He was taking a school trip with his class when a big truck on the other side of the road lost control and hit his bus."

"You lost a lot," MJ said, because she knew it was true and she didn't know what else to say about such terrible things.

"Sí," Papi agreed. "But they lost more. I'm still here."

"I guess . . . it's good you have so many other kids, right? At the school?"

Papi nodded. "It helps. It was the only thing that helped, really."

"I like Corrina a lot more than Stevie Lord," MJ said when she couldn't think of anything else to add to their current topic. "She's my favorite."

"I'm proud of her. Her mama wasn't always sure she'd turn out so well. I could tell you stories about her before she started training."

MJ's eyes lit up. "Oh yeah?"

They arrived at Victory Academy and as they climbed out of his truck, Papi began telling MJ about Corrina taking her mother's car without permission before she even had a driver's license. The darkness of the past few minutes started to leave him, and as they walked across the parking lot he was laughing about how mad Corrina's mother had been.

Almost as soon as they entered the school, MJ felt Papi's mood change again. He suddenly stopped walking with her, and when she looked up at him, he had an expression on his face almost as sour as the one he'd worn when they first met after he'd come back from his grandson's funeral.

He was staring hard across the warehouse and MJ looked to see what had gotten his attention. There was a man she hadn't seen at the school before. He was holding a leather notepad and a pen. It looked like he was inspecting all the Academy's equipment.

No one was training, MJ noticed. The students in attendance at Victory Academy that day were all gathered around the rings, just watching the man walk around the school and scribble in his pad.

"Wait here," Papi told her.

Papi stepped forward and smiled as he shouted across the warehouse at the man, "You took last week off!"

MJ could tell Papi was being fake nice.

"I was on vacation," the man said, sounding even more fake and wearing an equally phony smile that made MJ want to squirm.

"Where'd you jet off to?" Papi asked.

"Took the wife down to Cabo for our anniversary."

Papi walked over to him. They didn't shake hands. They just stared at each other, wearing their insincere smiles.

MJ studied the man Papi was talking to. He was shorter than Papi, and younger, with heavily greased black hair threaded with gray and a thin mustache and beard just around his chin. He was wearing a suit and tie, but it somehow looked wrong on him. MJ thought the man looked like a little kid wearing his father's suit to the school dance. His shoes were bright and shiny, but in an annoying way that made them distracting.

"So what's the damage going to be today?" Papi asked.

The man tore a page out of his notepad. "I guess me being away made you sloppy, Álvaro. The safety mats around your practice rings are worn thin and insufficient. You have some mold in the public restrooms. The power strips those vending machines are hooked up to are completely overloaded and a fire hazard—"

"So you're the fire chief now, too, Corto?" Papi interrupted him.

The man frowned, but it quickly turned into a sweet smile.

"Oh, and I noticed about a hundred holes poked in your air-conditioning unit."

Mr. Arellano's eyes went wide. "A hundred *what*? How does *that* happen?"

He looked around in shock and anger as if he expected one of the students or staff to answer him.

Everyone looked just as confused as he was, though.

Corto shrugged. "Maybe you have very precise rats. Either way, it's a violation and you'll have to replace it."

"Do you have any idea how much a new unit will cost?"

"Yes," Corto said as he stuffed the page he'd torn from his pad into Papi's hand.

Papi closed his fist around it angrily.

"I'll see you next week," he said, and even though his voice didn't get louder, it sounded like he wanted to scream. "Welcome back."

The man bowed his head, but like the rest of their exchange MJ could tell there was no respect in the gesture.

MJ, along with the rest of the students, watched silently

as he left their school. As he passed her, his shiny shoes clacked loudly on the cement floor.

MJ waited until he was gone, and then she jogged over to Papi, who was staring with a deep frown at the paper he'd been handed.

"Who was that?" she asked.

"His name is Neal Corto, and he works for the State Athletic Commission."

"What's that?"

"If you want to put on a boxing or a wrestling show in California, they have to say it's okay and give you a license. The same goes for running a school like Victory Academy."

"He doesn't seem to like you very much," MJ observed.

Papi laughed bitterly. "He hates wrestling. *Hates* it. If it were up to him there wouldn't be any wrestling in California at all. We're just the biggest and best school around, that's all."

"What did he want?"

Papi held up the slip of paper Corto had shoved into his hand before he left.

"This is a fine I have to pay for breaking their rules. Almost every week that . . ."

Papi made that face adults made when they were about

to say a curse word then realized MJ was standing there.

She wasn't a big fan of that face and wished they would all just say what they meant.

"He comes in here and finds any little thing he can make into a violation. Then he fines me for them. If he can't find a violation, he's good at making them up."

MJ was outraged. "That's not right!"

Papi shrugged. "He's got the badge. I mean, it's more like a laminated ID card, but it lets him do what he wants, just the same."

"Doesn't that cost you a lot of money?"

Papi sighed heavily. "A *lot* of money. I think that's why he does it. He's hoping he can bankrupt me out of here. And now I have to replace the air conditioner on top of it. Where did those holes come from?"

The first part of what he said scared MJ. "He won't, will he? Close down the school, I mean?"

He looked down at her, and seeing her concern seemed to melt away his anger. He smiled warmly.

"No, mija. They would have to burn this place down to get me out."

MJ nodded, trying to smile back. The thought of something, *anything* happening to the school still disturbed her.

"It'll take more than Mr. Neal Corto and his pad of tickets."

"So he's a rudo," MJ said.

Papi grinned bitterly. "That's right. He's definitely our bad guy."

YOUNG GIRLS

MJ couldn't believe the boards they bumped on every day were so heavy. Tika had explained to her what a ring was made of—the layers of canvas and foam over solid wood planks resting on a metal frame—but actually holding and carrying the end of one of those boards made her wonder why falling on them didn't hurt a lot more.

Zina was sixteen feet in front of her holding the other end, helping MJ carry it through Victory Academy's tall metal door that rolled up from the ground. Mr. Arellano had bought a new ring, and the younger and newer students were helping carrying it inside, piece by piece, where it would be put together.

The work was hard, but MJ didn't mind it so much.

She didn't mind doing anything, as long as she was at the school. What made it more difficult was the more experienced wrestlers who were training at Victory Academy that day. They all seemed to be assembled outside, sitting on the hood of someone's car and drinking water and Gatorade while they watched MJ and the others unload the ring.

They thought it was pretty funny, apparently. They were making jokes, and every now and then they shouted a few words of encouragement at the kids, and all laughed.

MJ couldn't decide whether it made her feel mad or embarrassed or both.

"Are they gonna help?" MJ asked Zina after they'd stacked the board they were carrying on the floor inside the school.

"Nah, workers don't do this stuff. This is what they have young boys for."

"Young boys?"

"It's like, a Japanese thing? The wrestlers who are just starting out, they're like assistants to the older wrestlers. They carry their bags and do chores for them and bring them stuff. They call them 'young boys.'"

"But we're girls."

"Then I guess we're young girls."

"Whatever. Feels pretty unfair to me."

Zina shook her head, waving at their audience as they

walked outside to get the next board.

"They all did it too," she explained to MJ. "They used to be us. And we'll be them one day."

"When?"

Zina laughed. "Sooner and not later, I hope."

"And then we'll have our own young girls?"

"Yup. It's the circle of life, like in *The Lion King*."

"I never saw it," MJ said.

Zina just stared at her. "Get Disney+, girl."

"I feel like you just told me to google it."

"I kinda did, but I didn't mean it ugly."

MJ believed that. Zina hadn't talked down to her or made fun of her once since they met.

They finished stacking the boards, and by the end of it, MJ had almost learned to tune out the people watching them and making jokes.

They were both tired and breathing hard, and their arms felt pulled out like taffy.

"I'll get us drinks," Zina told her.

"Thanks, young girl."

Zina flashed a deathly stare at her, but she also grinned.

MJ grinned back, watching her jog away to the vending machines.

While she waited, MJ took off her shoes and stepped

onto one of the practice mats that were always spread out across the school floor like spilled puzzle pieces. She shook out her arms and legs, flexing them until they felt strong again. Breathing in and out deeply, she set herself, turning to one side, planting her feet, and straightening her back.

MJ dipped her head and cartwheeled three times in a row over the mat. After the third cartwheel, she turned her body and faced the direction from which she'd come, launching into a standing back tuck. She flipped all the way over and landed smoothly on her feet.

She didn't really think about any of it. It was just something she did, the way other people looked at their phones when they were bored or waiting.

"That was *sick*!" she heard Zina yell.

MJ looked up and saw the older girl watching her with wide eyes and a smile, holding two bottles of Gatorade in her hands.

MJ smiled nervously and looked down at her feet.

"I used to do gymnastics, is all," she said.

"Used to? Why used to?"

MJ shrugged. "I didn't go out this year."

"Why not?"

"The other girls . . . one girl, really, but she's like, the boss chick of them all . . . she didn't like me. She made it hard."

"You tell me her name and I'll go kick her butt right now."

MJ laughed nervously. She knew Zina was joking, but it made her happy the other girl said that.

Zina grinned at her.

"What was her problem?"

"I don't know. She talked a lot of smack about Mexicans. I guess she didn't like one on her team."

"And *clearly* showing her up on the mat, from what I just saw."

"Maybe," MJ said, because that was as close to agreeing about her skills out loud as she could manage.

"I don't believe that you let some Becky keep you from doing something you're good at. You're tougher than that."

MJ shook her head. "I'm not, though. I'm . . . it's different at school than it is here."

"Still," Zina insisted.

"Other stuff happened," MJ said, quietly. "A lot of stuff."

"Like what?"

MJ swallowed. "Papi . . . my dad . . . he . . . left."

Zina frowned, her eyes somehow looking softer to MJ.

"Your mom and dad got divorced?"

MJ looked at the floor. She didn't want to explain. Saying he left was so much easier, but she liked Zina a lot, and she didn't want to lie to her.

"No," MJ said quietly. "He died."

"Omigod I'm sorry," Zina said quickly, and she really sounded like she was, both for MJ's loss and for pressing her to explain it.

She set the bottles she was holding down on the floor and reached out to stroke the upper part of MJ's arm.

"I didn't get it. I'm really sorry."

"It's okay."

MJ sniffed. Her voice was shaky, but it held together, and so did she. Zina's hand on her arm helped. It was almost like there was extra strength running from her hand into MJ's body.

"He loved wrestling," she said. "He was the one who showed it to me when I was little. We always watched it together."

Zina nodded sympathetically, not saying anything, just listening.

"He wouldn't have even believed this, what I'm doing. He would've *loved* all this."

That's when the tears started to come, but MJ shut her

eyes tight and sucked the tears back through her nose.

Zina full-on hugged her then, as tightly as MJ's abuelita would have.

Just like her hand on MJ's arm, it helped her keep herself from losing it.

"He sees you," Zina assured her, whispering. "From somewhere."

MJ hoped so. She didn't know for sure, but she hoped—more than just about anything—that Zina was right.

POWER SESSION

MJ had gone into great and colorful detail when describing the training sessions at Victory Academy to her mother. She wanted her mother to feel like she knew everything that was going on with MJ and the wrestling school, mostly so she would never feel the need to actually come and watch a class.

Because of her mother's schedule, she caught a break for the first several weeks that she attended the Academy. Since her father passed, her mother had been working weekends at a clothing store. That was on top of her regular office job and going to night school.

That finally changed one Saturday when another clerk, who badly needed extra money, asked to cover MJ's mother's shift at the store. Her mother agreed, and decided that since she had the day off, she would come to Victory Academy to watch MJ train.

MJ tried to talk her out of it. She told her mom she should call one of the friends she'd barely seen since the funeral, that she should go out with people other than MJ for a change and do something fun.

That wasn't just about stopping her from coming to MJ's wrestling class, either. She knew her mother needed to be around people more. For whatever reason, she didn't want to see Papi's family, no matter how many of them called or messaged her on Facebook. And her own parents had died before MJ was born.

Like most adults, however, Mom didn't listen to her. She'd decided to come to practice, and that was that. And, unfortunately, her mother chose a Saturday class that Mr. Arellano decreed would be a "power session."

Creepshow was leading the class. The purpose of a power session was for the more advanced students to work on their power moves, the higher-impact versions of slams and suplexes they used in their matches.

To help make the practice moves as much like executing them in a real match as possible, they "fed" the newer students to their more advanced peers to slam and suplex repeatedly. Even though they put foam-padded mats on top of the ring canvas to make it easier on the students taking all the moves, power sessions were tough to go through, and they were brutal to watch.

This all meant that instead of her mother seeing MJ take simple bumps and work on wrestling holds and running the ropes, she was about to watch MJ be pounded into the canvas over and over again.

That worried MJ.

It worried her a lot.

Mr. Arellano had brought her mother a folding chair to sit on, as well as a free soda. He was as cordial and gentlemanly as he was when he had first visited their home.

MJ was sitting on the apron of the training ring next to Zina, both waiting for their turns to be used as human punching bags. They could feel and hear the impact of the power moves being delivered in the ring behind them. MJ didn't want to see it. She was already nervous enough.

Zina was telling her all about Janelle Monáe, whose music MJ had never listened to before. Zina had been telling her about Janelle Monáe for the last ten minutes, in fact. MJ would normally have been fascinated, but she was so distracted by her mother being there and how she was going to react to what was about to happen.

"And it's like, everyone online or whatever talks about how brilliant Donald Glover is, and he's fine and all, but his stuff is so *basic* next to Janelle, you know? And how is she not the one hosting *Saturday Night Live* and having her own show and all that? She's like a goddess from another planet that's made of glitter and also everyone there is a genius."

"Right," MJ said, watching her mother watch the power session.

She seemed to be taking it well, at least.

MJ figured that would change when it was her daughter in there being slammed a million times in a row.

"*Dirty Computer* reminds me a lot of anime I've seen, actually. Do you watch anime?"

"Uh . . . I played like, Pokémon Go a lot when it came out, but then . . . a bunch of stuff happened, and I kind of stopped."

"You should check out *Wanna Be the Strongest in the World*. It's about Japanese women wrestlers. They call Japanese women's wrestling Joshi. They're like the baddest women workers in the world. Seriously. The show is about them. All the girls' boobs are huge, because anime, but it's *really* good."

"I don't know if my mom will let me watch that."

"Right. I see most of this stuff 'cuz of my brothers. Plus other stuff I do *not* want to see, honestly. Men are gross."

MJ laughed a little bit at that. It was almost enough to take her mind off her mother.

Creepshow leaned over the top rope above them.

"You two ready to take some bumps?"

Zina practically leaped to her feet on the apron, dipping through the ropes to step into the ring.

MJ hesitated, again glancing at her mother.

Creepshow noticed how uncomfortable she looked.

"¿Qué pedo?" he asked.

MJ didn't recognize the expression, but she knew enough to guess he was asking her what was wrong.

"My mom hasn't watched a class yet, and she was really nervous and weird about me coming here. I'm afraid if she sees me taking powerslams and stuff she's not going to let me train anymore."

Creepshow nodded, looking over at MJ's mother. The expression on his face turned serious, and MJ felt like he really understood why she was worried.

"Well, she's gotta see you train some time, or she'll just keep on stressing her and you about it."

Then his expression changed. He smiled big and bright and waved excitedly at her mother, who smiled and waved back.

"Don't worry about it," he urged her. "I got you."

MJ didn't know what that meant, but it did give her some hope.

She climbed through the ropes and stood behind Zina. MJ watched as the first student whipped Zina into the ropes and scooped her up as she ran back at him, power-slamming her down onto the foam padding. The handful of wrestlers in the class, a mix of men and women, all took turns suplexing or slamming her, and then it was MJ's turn.

She barely felt the big bumps, honestly. MJ couldn't stop thinking that after watching the session, her mother wouldn't want her wrestling anymore.

After the tenth or eleventh power move, MJ found herself lying facedown on the pads, breathing hard, and slow to get back to her feet. She didn't want to look at her mother, but she had to see her reaction.

To her surprise, MJ's mother barely seemed to be paying attention. Creepshow had sat down next to her, and the two of them looked like they were deep in conversation. MJ couldn't hear what they were saying, but after almost every sentence Creepshow spoke, her mother burst out laughing.

MJ couldn't believe it. After all her mother's complaining and refusing and worrying, and after finally insisting on coming to check out the class, she wasn't even watching MJ train.

It was the weirdest thing to MJ, but it also made her smile. She hadn't seen her mother laugh like that since Papi died.

Eventually Creepshow seemed to politely excuse himself from their chat. He stood up and walked back to the ring, clapping his hands loudly.

"Okay!" he announced. "Everybody take a break!"

Just like that, it was over.

MJ rolled out of the ring. Her body felt like it was made of wet noodles, but she forced herself to walk straight and tall and not let that feeling show even a little.

Her mother stood up from the chair, beaming at her.

"You did so good!" she announced to the whole school.

Besides being embarrassed by the volume of her voice, MJ still couldn't believe it.

"You uh . . . you were watching? The whole time?"

"Of course! You looked just like those girls on your wrestling shows!"

MJ didn't say anything else. She didn't want to push her luck.

"Can I stay to watch the Saturday night show?" she asked instead. "I told you about them, remember?"

"I don't know. I have class tonight."

"Mr. Arellano will take me home after."

"Maya, he's not your chauffeur."

"He doesn't mind! He lives right next door!"

Her mother sighed, but MJ knew that meant she was going to say it was okay.

"Fine," her mother finally relented. "Just don't get in his way, and you make sure you tell him thank you for being so kind to you."

"I will! I promise!"

MJ's mother looked back at the ring, which was empty now except for Creepshow. He was taking the opportunity while everyone else was cooling down to practice his own moves. He was rolling forward over his left shoulder, back and forth across the ring, popping up to his feet each time. He was so fast, and his every movement looked smooth.

MJ's mother had gotten quiet, and as she continued watching Creepshow she seemed to be thinking. MJ couldn't guess about what, but she really seemed lost in her thoughts.

"What's that boy's name again?" her mother asked. "Hernán?"

She pronounced his name almost like *Herman*, in that flat way she had with Spanish. MJ's father always made fun of how "white" her mother sounded when she said his relatives' names. They used to laugh about it.

"Yeah," MJ confirmed.

"He's *so* nice," her mother said, and there was a big,

goofy smile on her face as she said it.

MJ turned her head away to hide her grin.

"Yeah, he's really cool," she agreed.

MJ almost added that he was handsome too, just to tease her mother, but she didn't.

For one thing, MJ didn't want to think about her mom finding other guys handsome.

For another thing, thinking about how handsome Creepshow actually was made *her* feel weird and uncomfortable.

MJ didn't want to talk to her mom about that, either.

✦ ✦ ✦ ✦ ✦ ✦ ✦ ✦ ✦ ✦

THE DISASTER SHOW

The whole mess started with Jason Killgore and his run-in with a steel chair.

Actually, when they all thought later about that night, it really started with a call Papi received an hour before the show from Hector and three other students of the school. Hector told Papi that the group of them had taken a day trip to Disneyland. They had planned to be back in plenty of time for the show, but their car broke down on the freeway. To make things worse, the tow truck they called to rescue the foursome couldn't get to them because of a big accident on the same freeway a few miles away from where they had broken down.

Hector and the others would never make it in time for

the show. All four students had matches scheduled in the mid-card. There were only seven matches booked for the Saturday night show at the school, so it was like pulling the middle pages out of a novel. There were other newer students like MJ there at the show, but Papi only thought two of them were ready to have a real match, and he didn't look happy about it. That left them a match short before the show even started.

MJ was there to help set up the chairs and get the school ready to receive the crowd that came to watch the show. She was excited to watch the students and wrestlers she'd met actually work real matches.

Even better than that, Corrina Que Rico was there to perform. She wrestled on the shows when she had time off from Lucha Dominion. She held the Victory Academy Women's Championship.

"She's my favorite," MJ had explained to Zina as the two of them unfolded chairs and arranged them in rows around the middle ring.

"She's dope," Zina agreed. "I don't watch Lucha Dominion all the time, but I love watching her work here."

Papi had told MJ that the two most important matches on any card were the opener and the closer, the first match of the night and the last match, the main event. The last match was like the ending of a movie; it had to leave the crowd feeling satisfied. The first match was different. It set the tone for the show. If it was fast and entertaining, the crowd would be excited for everything that followed. If the first match was slow and boring, you'd have to work even harder to get the crowd's attention.

Corrina Que Rico was wrestling Duchess for the women's championship in the main event, so Papi had decided to begin the night's show with the second most popular rivalry in the school. Jason Killgore had been feuding with Creepshow on and off for the past year between Creepshow's stints in Japan. They had really convinced the crowd they hated each other, and everyone loved watching them brawl. Papi had also told MJ the key to a great feud was to keep building it. You had to make sure the next fight was different and more intense than the last, and you had to keep surprising the crowd.

For that night's opening match, Creepshow came to the ring first. Instead of waiting for his entrance music and the announcer, Papi told Killgore to run down the aisle with a folded-up steel chair, slide into the ring, and whack Creepshow with the chair before the bell to start the match even rang. MJ learned when one wrestler ambushed another wrestler it was called a "run-in." Everyone thought it was a good idea, and that it would start the match, and the show, "hot," at least that's the way Papi described it.

Unfortunately, it didn't go the way he had planned.

They had a good crowd that night. MJ peeked through the black curtains where the wrestlers made their entrances. She counted almost sixty people, and Papi told her that was a lot for a weekly show at a school. He told her there was a time when they were lucky to get twenty or thirty people at a show, but indie wrestling had been making a comeback over the past few years, and people were interested again.

The school's ring announcer was a local radio DJ who called himself Mo Love. He wore a tuxedo and slicked his hair back, and he had a voice that sounded like the guy who spoke over movie trailers. MJ thought he looked impressive, but all the wrestlers seemed to give him a hard time.

"How's everybody feelin' tonight?" he asked the crowd once he was standing inside the ring, speaking into a handheld microphone.

The people in the audience clapped and cheered. Many of them, MJ knew, were the family and friends of wrestlers who had matches on the card.

"I want to thank everyone for coming out and supporting these great up-and-coming talents here at Victory Academy. You're going to be seeing these guys and girls on your TVs one day soon, I promise you, and you'll be able to say, 'I saw them in a little gym in Mecca before they were famous! I was close enough to get sweat on me!'"

A few people in the crowd chuckled, and not enthusiastically.

"Our first match is scheduled for one fall with a fifteen-minute time limit. Introducing first, from the Castle Rock Cemetery, weighing two-hundred-and-thirty-two pounds . . . CREEPSHOW!"

A heavy metal song played and Creepshow burst through the curtains. The crowd started booing him, and he egged them on as much as he could, rolling inside the ring and climbing up the turnbuckles to yell at them through his mask and making big, insulting gestures with his hands.

Creepshow's entrance song hadn't even finished playing when Jason Killgore, a folded-up steel chair under one arm, ran through the curtain and sprinted down the aisle.

For some reason, instead of sliding inside the ring underneath the bottom rope with the chair, Killgore decided it would be more dramatic to throw the chair over the top rope and then slide into the ring and pick up the chair before he ambushed Creepshow.

At least, that was his plan.

Killgore reared back and threw the chair up at the top rope, but his aim was too low. Instead of sailing over the top rope and landing on the canvas, the chair bounced off the ropes and flew right back at Killgore. It was like someone launched it at him from a giant slingshot. The chair hit him in the face, making a sound like a frying pan hitting the floor. Killgore put his hands over his mouth and nose and backed up like he'd lost his balance, then he dropped to both knees.

Papi had a camera set up on top of the entrance, above where the curtains hung. It let everyone in the back watch the show on a big TV he had hung on the wall. When the chair smacked Killgore in the face, someone behind MJ yelled a word she wasn't allowed to use at home. The rest of the students and wrestlers gasped. She looked over at Papi, who didn't say a word, but the many lines in his stony face looked even deeper as he frowned at the screen.

Creepshow slid outside the ring and began dropping forearms across Killgore's shoulders. Even MJ could tell he was being gentle on Killgore, knowing he was really hurt, but Creepshow was trying to cover up what was going on and hide it from the crowd. He grabbed Killgore and pulled him to his feet. He did his best to make it look like they were fighting up the entrance aisle, but what he was really doing was helping Killgore make it to the back.

Once they were behind the curtains, Papi walked over to Killgore and pulled his hands away from his face roughly, forcing the young wrestler to tilt his head back.

"Oh my god!" MJ squeaked before she could stop herself.

Killgore's nose looked like her mother's huevos rancheros. There was blood streaking down his neck and chest. Creepshow helped him to sit in one of the same kind of chairs that had just destroyed his face.

Creepshow pushed his mask up over his forehead. His real face was full of concern for the other wrestler.

"I think his nose is broken," he said.

"Of course it's broken," Papi said. "He tried to make out with a steel chair."

"I'm sorry, Papi," Killgore said, although it sounded like he was trying to talk around a mouth full of cereal.

"Don't talk," the old man instructed him.

"I didn't know what else to do," Creepshow said, sounding worried that he'd messed up too.

"You did good," Papi told him, his voice less harsh than when he spoke to Killgore.

Then, raising his voice so everyone else could hear, he said, "Did everyone see that? What do I always tell you? Mess up, cover up. You always have to be thinking out there. Don't stop just because something goes wrong. Think of a way out and keep going. And you watch out for the other worker in the ring with you. Always."

Someone brought Papi a first aid kit and the old man opened it and ripped open the package of a compress to put over Killgore's nose.

"Get the next match going," he instructed the rest of them.

The second match was the first women's bout of the night, featuring Tika. MJ didn't know the name of her opponent, a lanky blonde girl who went out first, and she missed hearing Mo Love announce it because MJ was watching Mr. Arellano patch up Killgore.

"Papi!" one of the students yelled. "We got another one down!"

MJ turned her head to look at the monitor. The blonde girl had fallen right in front of the ring. She was holding her head as if she'd hit it on the ground.

"You've gotta be kidding me," Tika said, watching what just happened on the monitor.

"What'd she slip on?" somebody asked.

MJ squinted at the monitor. "Um . . . I think it's blood."

Killgore's broken nose must have bled onto the cement floor in front of the ring.

Papi rushed out through the curtain, and they all watched as he tended to the girl. After a few minutes, he walked her back behind the curtain. She seemed dazed, but she was conscious and she was answering questions.

She couldn't wrestle, though.

They were now over twenty minutes into the show and not only had they failed to put on even one match, the first five matches Papi booked couldn't happen.

"We could put somebody under a hood and have them work double duty," Tika suggested.

"Does anybody have a spare gimmick?" Papi asked everyone in the back.

No one spoke up.

Papi sighed heavily. "*Nobody* has a spare gimmick? How about training gear that's the same color? Anything?"

The old man shook his head in disbelief.

"I have my new rash guard," MJ said without even thinking about it. "It looks pretty cool."

As soon as the words left her mouth, she wished she could take them back. All eyes in the room turned to her in the next moment, and then half of the people who were looking at her started to laugh.

The staring was bad enough. The laughter was worse.

"I'll work her," Tika said suddenly, and that quieted everyone.

"She's a baby and she's green on top of it," someone said.

"I've been training with her," Tika told him. "She can make it through one match."

Tika's confidence gave MJ a thrill, but she still felt embarrassed with everyone's attention on her, especially Papi's.

He was staring down at her with a serious look on his face. Then he looked over at Tika with the same expression.

"If you think you can lead her through a match, fine," he said, but he didn't sound all the way convinced. "But it's on you."

Tika just nodded without saying anything in reply.

"Go change," Papi ordered MJ. "Be quick about it."

Her legs felt like jelly suddenly, but MJ took off running anyway. She sprinted to the locker room where her bag was waiting and changed into her rash guard and tights. She was back in less than two minutes, already out of breath.

Papi, Creepshow, Tika, and Corrina were all standing together in the back, talking about her.

"We can't have a twelve-year-old wrestling Tika," Creepshow said. "It's going to look stupid, like she's beating up her little sister."

He thought about what he'd just said for a second, and then he looked at MJ.

"No offense, kid," he told her, and he sounded like he meant it.

MJ shrugged. She didn't know what else to do.

When she looked back up at Papi he seemed to be

thinking about Creepshow's words.

Slowly, he walked over to a trunk in the corner and opened the lid. He dug around inside of it for several seconds, and then suddenly stopped. He was staring into the trunk with such a sad look on his face, MJ thought. Then Papi reached back inside and picked up something. He removed it carefully, like it might break if he was too rough with it. When he held it up it was almost like he was holding some sacred object.

It was a máscara, a real luchador's mask. However, this was the smallest lucha mask MJ had ever seen. It looked like it was made for a kid. The mask was shiny and blue, like the sun's light bouncing off the ocean, and it had bright yellow lightning bolts sewn to both sides of its head.

MJ wasn't sure how, but she felt the mood in the entire back room change. She looked around at the faces of all the wrestlers and students, and most of them were wearing sad and surprised looks.

Papi handed the mask to MJ.

"Try this on," he told her. "If they can't see your face you'll just look little instead of young. Like you said, you're as tall as Rey Mysterio."

He smiled as he said that last part, just a little, but he still looked sad to MJ.

She took the mask from him, being as careful as he'd

been when he removed it from the trunk. It had laces all up and down the back, and the strings hung loosely from it. MJ carefully slid the mask over her head and face, but it fit awkwardly. It wasn't the size that was the problem; her long hair was bound up in a ponytail, and that ponytail was pushing against the back of the mask.

Corrina Que Rico noticed the problem and walked over to MJ.

"We need to do something about that," she said, and then looked at Papi. "Is it okay if I . . .?"

Papi didn't answer her at first. He had a very odd look on his face.

Finally, he shrugged. "Do what you need to do."

After he said that he turned and walked away from them.

Corrina went over to her gear bag and took out a folding knife. She snapped it open with an expert flick of her wrist.

"Turn around and don't move," she instructed MJ, who did exactly as she was told.

Corrina carefully cut a small hole in the back of MJ's hood, near the top of her head, then pulled MJ's ponytail through it. With that done, she was able to quickly lace up the mask so it fit tightly but comfortably on MJ's head. She finished by tying off the laces in a tiny bow.

Corrina stepped back to look at MJ and grinned. "That's *hype*, mija!"

"You look good," Tika said. "What are we going to call you?"

"What else?" Corrina said with another grin. "Chica Relámpago."

MJ tried, but she couldn't make her brain translate the last word.

Corrina could see she was confused.

"Lightning Girl," she explained. "That's you."

"It'll do," Papi said from across the room. "For now. I'll go tell Mo. Pick her out some music and get it ready."

He left the back and slipped out through the curtain.

"What's wrong with him?" MJ asked the two of them when she was sure Papi was too far away to hear.

"This mask was his grandson's," Tika told her quietly.

"They called him Chico Relámpago," Corrina added. "Lightning Boy."

MJ's eyes went wide. She finally understood why Papi was acting so strange.

"Maybe I shouldn't—" she started to say, but Corrina shook her head and waved at her to stop.

"It's a good way to honor him," she insisted. "That mask belongs on a luchador—"

"Or luchadora," Tika added.

Corrina nodded. "And not at the bottom of a trunk. It's good for Papi, too. Even if it doesn't feel like it right now. It'll help him move on."

MJ wasn't so sure, but she didn't say it.

Corrina left her and Tika to let them get ready for their match and to go pick out music for MJ, to play as she entered the ring.

"Do you want to talk about what moves you want to do?" MJ asked Tika, trying to keep her voice from sounding shaky and nervous.

Tika grinned. "Don't worry about remembering anything right now. Just do what I tell you out there and remember your bumps, okay? And when I tell you to 'go home,' that means don't kick out when I pin you. Understand?"

MJ nodded her head faster and longer than she meant to, but she couldn't help it. All she could feel was excitement mixed with fear making her body feel like electricity was going through it.

Papi returned to the back. He didn't look at MJ as he walked over to the school's sound system. There was an MP3 player hooked up to the controls, and Corrina was scrolling through the songs on it.

"Just pick something," MJ heard him tell her, and he sounded impatient and more than a little annoyed.

"¡Cálmese!" Corrina fired back at him and she continued to scroll through the MP3 player.

MJ had noticed Corrina was one of the few people in the school who Papi couldn't shake up, even when he was really mad. In fact, nothing seemed to shake up Corrina.

MJ silently hoped she could be like that one day.

"Here we go!" Corrina announced. "I found a good Tejano rock track for you, mija."

"Just get it ready," Papi muttered.

MJ took a deep breath.

"Don't worry," Tika said, squeezing MJ's shoulder. "You'll be fine. Just remember what I told you."

MJ tried to say that she'd remember, but the words stuck in her throat and she just coughed and nodded again.

Tika laughed, but it didn't make MJ feel embarrassed, like Tika was laughing *at* her. There was just something kind about the older girl that made MJ feel comfortable and safe. It was a nice change from being at her other school where she felt the opposite way most of the time.

Mo Love introduced MJ first.

"Weighing in at one hundred and thirty-three pounds, from Guanajuato, Mexico . . . CHICA RELÁMPAGO!"

It took MJ a few seconds to realize Mo was talking about *her*. That wasn't where she was from, and that was way more than she weighed. Was MJ supposed to look bigger? How did you make yourself look bigger, she wondered. No one had taught her how to do that, and not knowing caused her heart to pound even harder.

All that new uncertainty made her think of something else. She was supposed to be Lightning Girl, but she didn't know who Lightning Girl was. She only knew who MJ was, and when she walked out there, she wasn't supposed to be MJ anymore. She didn't know whether Lightning Girl was good, bad, or in-between. What was she supposed to *do* when she wasn't taking bumps in the ring? How was she supposed to act?

There was no time to ask anyone else. There wasn't even time to think more about it. Her music was playing, and Mo had introduced her. She had to go.

When she walked out through the curtain, no one in the crowd made any noise, even though they were all looking at her. It made MJ feel even more nervous and embarrassed. She tried to push all those feelings down deep inside her and just think about wrestling.

Since the crowd liked Tika, MJ knew she should probably be the heel. She thought about all the bad guys and bad girls she saw on TV every week. Most of them would yell at the crowd, or get in their faces and threaten them, but MJ was too shy to do that. She didn't feel tough or mean as she walked down the aisle, she just felt everyone's eyes on her and it made her want to run the other way, through the curtain, back to where it was safe.

She didn't, of course. She couldn't. MJ had asked for this and Papi had given it to her. She couldn't let him down.

So instead, halfway down the aisle, MJ broke into a run and sprinted the rest of the way to the ring, sliding under the bottom rope. It felt good to move that fast. She felt like it burned away some of the nervousness she was feeling. When she popped up to her feet on the canvas her legs felt a little steadier, and her breathing wasn't so shaky.

MJ also found she felt better once she was in the ring. She didn't feel the eyes of the crowd burning into her the way she did when she walked down the aisle. It was almost like there was an invisible wall around the ring. She could still hear them, but even the sound of the crowd seemed quieter, and all the people felt far away. She couldn't see any of their faces. It was mostly dark outside of all the lights that were shining down on the ring.

The music they'd picked out for MJ ended and Tika's music started playing. People recognized it immediately, and she could hear them getting excited to see her.

"And her opponent!" Mo Love shouted into the microphone. "Weighing one hundred and fifty-seven pounds, from East Los! Tika Powers!"

Tika didn't just step from behind the curtains; she

burst out of them like she was breaking through a brick wall. She had a big, confident smile on her face. MJ watched Tika as the more experienced girl made her entrance. Tika stopped and flexed her thin but muscular arms for the fans with a smile, and they loved it.

MJ stood in one of the corners of the ring as Tika leaped up onto the apron and then launched herself over the top rope, landing on her feet like a gymnast posing for the Olympic judges.

Eventually the music stopped, and even the cheers of the fans faded. MJ's heart was beating so hard in her chest, she was sure everyone around her could hear it. She also felt her forehead sweating under her hood, and she hoped that it wasn't making a wet spot on top of the mask that the people could see.

The bell rang, signaling the start of the match, and even though it was just a tiny hammer hitting a rusted old piece of metal, it sounded like thunder in MJ's ears.

The ring seemed smaller somehow as she stared across at Tika and they began to circle. MJ watched Tika's feet, remembering to match the way she moved and keep up with her so they stayed facing each other.

They locked up. MJ found herself face to face with Tika, who winked at her with a grin.

"Just relax," she said so only MJ could hear her.

MJ told herself not to nod. No one was supposed to notice the two of them talking to each other.

Tika put MJ through a quick series of standing wrestling holds, folding and locking onto the younger girl's arm one way, then smoothly transitioning to another. MJ moved through her part of the holds mechanically, having no problem keeping up with Tika or remembering how each hold and transition worked. It made her feel more comfortable; these were holds she'd been drilling with Papi for weeks. MJ realized that's why Tika was doing it, to relax MJ and take her mind off being in her first match.

Tika ended the series by looping her arm around MJ's neck and putting her in a light headlock. Tika made a big show of wrenching the hold to make it seem like she was really putting pressure on MJ's head, though MJ didn't feel it.

Still holding onto the headlock, Tika dipped her own head forward and let her hair fall in front of her face to mask her mouth.

"Okay, push me off and I'll tackle you," Tika whispered to MJ.

MJ did as she was told, shoving Tika so that she let go of the headlock and ran to the ring ropes. Tika bounced off and came back at MJ with a shoulder tackle. MJ didn't fling herself back onto the mat. Instead, when their bodies connected, MJ let the impact and gravity do the work for her, falling naturally onto her back without fighting it. The first bump she'd taken in the match was jarring, even though MJ remembered to tuck her chin and slap out. It didn't hurt, but she felt it throughout her entire body, even on the tip of her tongue and the ends of her toes.

She looked up from where she lay on the ring floor and saw Tika motioning for her to get up. MJ quickly sprang to her feet. Tika didn't move toward her, so MJ ran at Tika, yelling out her best battle cry like she was going to attack the older girl furiously. MJ knew Tika would do something to cut MJ off, even if she didn't know what that would be. MJ kept reminding herself to just go with whatever Tika did, and to stay loose and relaxed.

Tika hooked her elbow around MJ's and arm-dragged her, making MJ somersault forward and flip onto her back. She'd spent so much time practicing rolling across the canvas and popping back up to her feet that MJ's body performed the action almost on its own, without her having to think about it. She knew Tika would want her to turn around and run back to take another move, so that's exactly what MJ did.

Instead, Tika smacked her on the behind, and though she hadn't been taught how to react, MJ had watched enough lucha libre to know she was supposed to run at the ring ropes and bounce off them so Tika could set up another move. MJ hit the ropes and ran back at Tika, who quickly stepped aside and pushed against the small of MJ's back with one hand. MJ sprinted faster and bounced off the ropes with even more speed this time. When she ran back at Tika again, the much more experienced girl leaned forward and lifted MJ up into the air with her arms and shoulders.

For a moment, the world around MJ slowed down. The ring floor seemed impossibly far away as she looked down at it. Tika pushed against her legs and MJ flipped over, her view of the canvas turning into a blinding look up at the lights. Everything sped back up to normal speed. Flying through the air higher than she yet had inside a wrestling ring was a thrill, like a tiny version of riding a roller coaster.

When MJ's back hit the canvas this time, she barely even felt it. She was breathing hard and fast, and she knew it wasn't from the bump or the small amount of running around she'd just done. It was her nerves.

Tika pulled MJ up and put her through a few more moves, including a big biel out of the corner that sent MJ flying halfway across the ring. Finally, Tika hooked her arm around the back of MJ's head and set her up for a suplex.

"We'll go home after this," she whispered to MJ before lifting her once more into the air.

She was practically gasping for breath after Tika dropped her on the mat for the last time. MJ couldn't believe how exhausted she was after what couldn't have been more than six or seven minutes in the ring. Between her nerves and grappling with Tika and taking so many bumps, MJ felt as though she'd just run a mile.

She waited. Tika was climbing up the turnbuckles to perform her finishing move, a big splash from the top rope. MJ actually felt a calm, cold relief rushing through her body. The match was all but over now. She just had to lie there and wait for Tika to leap and land on her. She had made it through this trial by fire.

She braced herself, remembering to be ready to slightly lift her top half off the canvas right before Tika landed to soften the impact.

Except Tika didn't come.

It had only been seconds since Tika left MJ lying there, but during a match seconds could seem like hours, especially when the action stopped. MJ felt those extra seconds stretching unusually long, and she knew Tika should've landed on her by now.

MJ looked over at the corner, confused. Then her confusion turned into alarm, and that turned into panic.

Tika had made it to the top turnbuckle, but she must have slipped. She was sitting awkwardly on the metal link that connected the buckle to the ring post. It looked like she was in real pain, and MJ could imagine why. She must have landed with that metal link between her legs. It made MJ shudder, thinking about how that had to feel.

MJ tried to tell herself to calm down. She would just wait, that's all. She would wait for Tika to climb back up and they would finish the match as planned. Tika was tough. Even if she were hurt, she would push through it. They only had to complete one last move, after all.

Those good thoughts gave her a short second of hope, but they quickly melted away when she saw Tika was still sitting on that metal link. She was squirming around, but not making any progress in climbing back up onto the top turnbuckle. Then MJ noticed why.

Tika's right boot seemed like it was caught between the turnbuckles. Though she was trying to pull it free, even though it looked like it hurt her to do so, she couldn't work it loose. Maybe her foot or her ankle was broken, MJ couldn't be sure.

Oh no, MJ thought. *She's stuck.*

Maybe she was just imagining it, but MJ thought she could hear the crowd getting restless and confused. They were starting to realize something wasn't right.

MJ had seen enough wrestling matches to know that when wrestlers fell on the top rope like that, their opponents would use the chance to climb up after them and take control of the fight.

Mess up, cover up, Papi's strong voice said inside her head.

MJ sprang to her feet. She took a deep breath and prepared to run into the corner where Tika was trapped. It surprised her to realize that her legs weren't shaking the way they had before the match started. She knew what she had to do, and she knew in that moment she could do it.

MJ took off running. Two feet in front of the corner she bent down and launched into the biggest jump her legs could muster. She cleared the bottom and second rope, then felt just the tips of her booted toes touch the top rope. For just a moment MJ panicked, certain she was about to slip and fall. She didn't, however. Somehow, by waving her arms in big circles and saying a silent prayer to the saints, whose candles her abuelita had taught her to light, MJ was able to balance on the top rope in front of where Tika was sitting.

"Jump up onto my shoulders and lock your legs together," Tika whispered urgently to MJ.

MJ didn't stop to think about it, she just did what she was told. Bouncing off the top rope, she jumped up and sat on Tika's shoulders, crossing her ankles against Tika's back. Tika grabbed her by the hips to steady her.

"Fall back and just let me guide you, okay?" she instructed MJ. "Keep your chin tucked."

MJ fell away from the top turnbuckle into a backflip, pulling Tika with her. It looked like she was using her legs to flip Tika forward, a lucha move invented by Huracán Ramírez. Instead of landing on her back on the canvas, however, Tika straightened herself out in the middle of the air. She was still holding MJ around her waist, and she pulled MJ into a second backflip.

MJ felt the world spin and spin around her, making her dizzy and confused, and then her back hit the canvas. Tika powerbombed her to the mat. It was the biggest bump MJ had ever taken, and it knocked all the air out of her. Oddly, she didn't really feel it. It didn't hurt, and she'd kept her chin tight to her chest, so she hadn't hit her head. It just made her body tense up, and after she landed, she found it was hard to make her muscles relax again.

Even as shaken as she was by the bump, MJ knew that she and Tika had just performed a spectacular move. She heard the crowd explode in shock and excitement, then all the sounds around her seemed to go quiet, and the only thing MJ could see was the bright lights overhead burning down on them. She felt something hitting the mat next to her and realized it was the referee's hand slapping the canvas as he counted one, two, and three.

The sound of a bell ringing was the next thing MJ really heard clearly. It was the ring bell signaling the end of the match. It was finally over. They'd only wrestled for seven or eight minutes, but to MJ it felt like an entire school year had gone by.

Tika untangled her body from MJ's and stood up to have her arm raised by the referee. MJ slowly rolled across the canvas, ducked under the bottom rope, and let her body drop to the protective foam mats that surrounded the ring. Not only had her breath come back after that big bump, but she was panting like a dog after a long run. She remembered what Papi and Tika had both told her about breathing, so she tried to slowly draw in air through her nose and then let it go through her mouth.

MJ wouldn't see the final move of the match until later, in the video. All she knew right then was whatever the move had been, it must have looked good to the people watching. The sound of the crowd cheering was like thunder. A hundred people sounded like thousands to MJ. It was the loudest by far they'd been since the show started.

She continued to lay there while Tika celebrated her victory and played to the crowd. She knew better than to just get up and walk away. She was supposed to be hurt from that huge powerbomb. She made sure to sell it as she half crawled, half staggered away from the ring, holding her neck and her back as if she were in great pain.

When she walked through the curtains and returned to the back, everyone started clapping and hooting for MJ. She was even less prepared for it than she was for the match before she had gone out there. It was like walking into a surprise party.

Tika soon joined her in the back, and she scooped up MJ in a bear hug, squeezing her so tight that the breath MJ had finally collected rushed right back out of her.

"So proud of you, girl!" Tika congratulated her as she released MJ.

The only person who wasn't smiling or applauding was Papi. He stood off to the side, thick arms folded across his wide chest, a sour look on his face.

He waited until everyone was done congratulating her and they'd all returned their attention to the show, then he walked over to her. He looked mad. MJ barely had time to feel happy about the reaction she'd just received before the feeling was replaced by something almost like fear.

Papi leaned down so only she could hear him.

"Don't ever do that again," he said in a heavy voice. "You could have broken your neck. You *should* have broken your neck. Don't ever confuse luck with skill. ¿Entiendes?"

MJ wanted to tell him that she was just doing what Tika told her to do like he'd instructed her, but she couldn't get any words out just then. She was too stunned by his reaction. She barely managed to nod.

He walked away from her to deal with starting the next match, leaving MJ feeling alone even though the room was filled with people still smiling at her with pride and affection.

That night MJ learned it didn't matter if a thousand people cheered for you as long as the one person whose opinion you cared about the most didn't.

PART TWO:
LIGHTNING GIRL

★ ★ ★ ★ ★ ★ ★ ★ ★ ★ ★

40,000 LIKES AND COUNTING

The week after her debut match, MJ's mother dropped her off at Victory Academy early Saturday morning.

"I want to come in and talk to that old man," her mother said as she parked the car in front of the main entrance to the school.

"Mom, no!" MJ pleaded, horrified by the thought of her doing that.

"I've been thinking about it, and we need to get a few more things straight about you coming here."

Her mother had been less than thrilled about MJ's in-ring debut. MJ had contemplated not telling her about the match with Tika, but she decided her mother would find out sooner or later, and it would be so much worse later.

"You should have asked me first," her mother insisted for probably the seventh time. "And he should have asked me, too."

"I already told you," MJ reminded her, "it was an *emergency*. There was no time. All I did was stuff I'd already learned how to do. Tika took care of me. It's not going to happen again. Papi didn't like me wrestling on the show so soon, anyway. You should have heard him."

Her mother had been staring out the window at the front of the school. Suddenly her gaze snapped to MJ. There was a strange, surprised look on her face.

"You call Mr. Arellano 'Papi?'"

"Oh," MJ said, only just realizing her mother hadn't known, and that it must be weird for her, just like it was for MJ at first.

"Everyone calls him that in the school," she explained. "It's like his nickname."

Her mother nodded, still looking surprised and unsure of how to react.

"Can I go in now, please?" MJ asked.

Her mother sighed, seeming to melt into her seat.

"Fine," she said tiredly. "But I want a full report on what happens in there from now on. You hear me?"

MJ nodded enthusiastically. "I swear."

Her mother waved her away, and MJ bolted from the car.

There were about a dozen students at the school already. They were easy to count because as MJ walked inside everyone was gathered into a tight circle in the common area by the vending machines. They all appeared to be staring at something MJ couldn't see from far away, and whatever it was, everybody seemed excited about it.

MJ started walking toward the group. When she was about halfway over to them, MJ heard somebody shout, "There she is!"

All heads turned in her direction, and MJ realized that they were talking about her.

She stopped walking. She was opening her mouth to ask what was going on when Tika's head popped up from the middle of the circle of people.

"Oh my god!" she yelled.

Tika began pushing her way out from the circle of bodies, and as they all stepped apart MJ could see that one of them was holding a phone playing a video. That's what they'd all been watching when MJ walked in.

"You're famous, girl!" Tika announced, smiling from ear to ear.

MJ thought Tika was talking to someone else for a

moment. MJ even looked behind her to see if anyone was there.

"What are you talking about?" she asked.

Tika snatched the phone away from the student holding it. She ran over to where MJ was standing to show her.

MJ was confused at first when Tika played back the YouTube clip on the phone's screen.

"Wait, is that me?" MJ asked, shocked. "Is that our match?"

"It's the last spot from our match," Tika explained.

It was. Someone in the crowd at last Saturday's show had recorded the end of their match on a phone and uploaded the clip. It was the move where MJ tried to take Tika over with her legs and Tika turned it into a powerbomb. MJ hadn't watched any video of the match yet, so it was the first time she'd been able to see how the move looked.

Even she had to admit, all those flips in midair and then the impact of the powerbomb looked pretty spectacular.

The title whoever had shot the video put on the clip was, "LITTLE GIRL LUCHADORA AMAZING WRESTLING MOVE!!!"

"Little girl?" MJ said with disdain.

Tika waved the words away. "Don't worry about that. Check out the views!"

MJ looked at where the viewer count was displayed.

The number represented how many times the video had been watched so far.

She blinked in disbelief as she saw that the clip had almost eight hundred thousand views already, and over forty thousand likes.

"Dude." MJ gasped.

Tika beamed. "I know, right?"

"I don't believe it."

"You've totally gone viral! In your first match!"

"That don't mean anything!" Mr. Arellano's voice boomed from across the school.

MJ looked up and saw him walking out from behind the show curtain, a stern and annoyed expression on his face.

"Oh, Papi, let her have this!" Tika shot back, unafraid. "She did good!"

"She shouldn't have been in the ring in the first place, and you should know better!"

In response, Tika stuck her tongue out at him.

MJ couldn't believe it. Just hearing him talk like that was making MJ's heart beat fast and she felt blood rushing hot between her ears. She couldn't imagine being as calm and unaffected by his reprimand as Tika appeared.

"You're just being a grouch," Tika chided him. "Besides, this is so good for the school and the Saturday shows!"

Mr. Arellano grunted. "It's the internet. It's not good for anything."

"Oh my god, you are so old." Tika breathed in frustration.

"Are you booking children on your shows now, Álvaro?"

MJ looked around to see who had asked that question, not recognizing the voice at first.

She almost jumped when she saw Corto. He'd slipped into the school quietly enough not to be noticed by any of them until he spoke. He was standing off to the side, holding that clipboard of his behind his back and staring at them all like they were animals in a zoo.

From the look in his eyes MJ would have guessed he hated the zoo.

"Weekly inspection time?" Mr. Arellano asked him sourly, and without bothering to make their usual sarcastic small talk.

Corto ignored the question. He was looking directly at MJ now, and it made her want to run away.

"Seriously though," he said, "are you having *that* much trouble finding gullible teenagers to toss in your meat grinder? What's next? Kindergartners?"

Mr. Arellano sighed tiredly. "Her mother signed the waiver when she joined," he said, talking about MJ. "The school shows are exhibitions. No one's getting paid. There are no rules against her wrestling on those cards."

"Not a good look, though," Corto said, finally taking his eyes off MJ to stare at Papi.

"Who's looking? You?" Mr. Arellano laughed bitterly, practically snorting. "You're *always* looking, and you never like what you see, so what difference does it make? Now, do you want to see the air conditioner? It cost me four grand to get it fixed for no reason."

Corto didn't answer at first. There was a weird look on his face, or at least MJ thought it was weird. It was like he was thinking really hard about something, but he didn't want any of them to know he was thinking.

"No," he finally said. "No, I think I've seen enough for today."

MJ could tell that surprised Papi. He stared back at Corto and frowned.

"Fine," he said. "Thanks for stopping by."

Corto left, but not before taking one last, long look at MJ.

"That guy sucks *so hard*," Tika said after he was gone, sounding like she wasn't concerned with what just happened, or how strange Corto was acting.

"Watch your mouth," Papi chastised her.

"*Anyway*, forget him." She held up the phone with the clip of MJ as Lightning Girl playing on it. "Look! There's a bunch of people in the comments who are local and they're asking where the school is so they can come to the show! And people are telling them to come to Victory Academy!"

"They're just student shows," Mr. Arellano insisted. "*Exhibitions*. Weren't you listening to what I just said to Corto? They're so you all can get practice in front of the crowd. That's all."

"Well, more people could come," Tika insisted. "And you need the money! *Especially* with that weasel fining us every week."

Mr. Arellano took a deep breath and dug his fists into his hips, resting them there.

"You're not as wrong as you usually are," he finally admitted.

Tika nodded triumphantly. "So, I have an idea."

Mr. Arellano groaned.

"Just listen!"

Despite feeling awkward that they were talking about her, and still thinking Papi was mad at her, MJ giggled at the exchange.

"Maya should be on the show again," Tika said.

That put an end to MJ's giggling.

"Huh?" she managed to blurt out.

"You should be on the show!" Tika repeated. "This video, this could be like your gimmick!"

"How can a YouTube video be a gimmick?" MJ asked.

Tika growled jokingly. "*Nobody* gets me! No, not the video! What happens *on* the video! That's your thing. You get beat up and you get beat up more and then you pull off a big, impressive spot and *almost* win, but it gets reversed."

"What in the world are you babbling about?" Mr. Arellano demanded.

"Papi, think about it!" Tika urged the old man. "She can do a squash match. You saw her. She bumped great for me. And the crowd freaked out! And everyone loves this clip!"

Mr. Arellano rubbed his head. "We *just* had that pendejo Corto in here giving me grief for booking her on the last show, so now you want me to book her on the *next* show?"

"You said yourself there are no rules against it, so who cares what he says? He hates us anyway!"

"I'm going to figure what you just said makes sense to you because you're so young."

"It's like an underdog gimmick, you know?" Tika persisted, ignoring him like she always did. "She's little and she gets squashed over and over, but then at the end she *almost* pulls out the win with a big spot. If we do it on every show, the people will start wanting to see her win. They'll keep hoping she pulls it off this time. Each match will build the anticipation. And then when she's ready and she finally goes over on somebody, they'll go nuts! Tell me that isn't a great gimmick! Go ahead, tell me!"

Mr. Arellano stared down at Tika like all he wanted was for her to suddenly disappear, or at least not be able to talk anymore, but to MJ's surprise he didn't tell her it was a bad idea.

MJ had listened while Tika explained her plan, getting more and more excited, but not because Tika was trying to get MJ more matches. It just sounded like a great wrestling story to her. It was almost like Tika was talking about someone else.

Then it hit her that Tika was telling Papi that MJ should be the one to do this.

Tika nudged MJ with her elbow.

"See that?" she said, nodding at Mr. Arellano. "His wrestling brain is kicking on."

"Don't tell me what I'm thinking, young lady," he chastised her. "My brain is three times as old as yours."

"But it's the same size," Tika reminded him.

Mr. Arellano swore under his breath in frustration.

"It's a good idea!" Tika pressed. "We'll at least get a few more people showing up who saw the video. Put her in a squash on the mid-card so people have to wait to see her.

That way they get to watch the other matches and see how good they are. If they see the rest of the show they'll definitely come back next week."

"You a worker or a booker now?" Mr. Arellano asked her sarcastically.

Tika pressed her lips together tightly, not saying anything more.

MJ had the thought that Tika knew she'd pushed the old man as far as she could.

Mr. Arellano looked down at MJ, almost as if he were sizing her up all over again.

"All right, Lightning Girl," he said a few moments later. "We'll try it. It'll be good bump training for you, anyway."

Tika practically squealed with delight.

Mr. Arellano wagged a thick finger at her. "You run whatever big spot you come up with by me first. No more surprises."

"Yes, Papi!" Tika shouted, jumping up to kiss him on the cheek.

MJ, on the other hand, was speechless.

Tika patted her on the cheek. "Hey, you in there? You're going to be on the show again!"

MJ managed to nod.

"So get your gear on and we'll figure out a new spot for tonight!"

Tika walked away from her, leaving MJ alone to soak in the impact of the past few minutes.

As much as the thought of wrestling more actual matches thrilled and scared her, it was nothing compared to how MJ felt inside at the thought of telling her mother.

★ ★ ★ ★ ★ ★ ★ ★ ★ ★ ★

HEAT

MJ stood in front of the Victory Academy bathroom mirror without really looking at her reflection and slipped the Lightning Boy hood over her head. She pulled her ponytail through the hole in the back before lacing the mask up tight. She adjusted it around her ears, nose, and eyes until it felt comfortable, and then she looked in the mirror.

She still didn't recognize her reflection, and the mask didn't look or feel like it belonged to her. She didn't feel like Chica Relámpago, Lightning Girl. She felt like a kid wearing someone else's mask and pretending to be a wrestler.

She wasn't going to tell anybody that, though.

She'd made the dreaded call to her mom and gotten

permission to wrestle another match. Despite how afraid MJ had been to talk to her, her mother was surprisingly calm about the whole thing.

Then her mother asked to speak to Mr. Arellano, and although the old man smiled all through the call, MJ was sure Mom spent the entire time yelling at him.

Her opponent was going to be Duchess, who'd wrestled and lost to Corrina the week before in a title match. The angle (which is what people in the business called a wrestling storyline) was going to be that Duchess was mad about losing and was going to take it out on MJ. The fact MJ was half the size of Duchess would only make the crowd hate her more.

MJ's big move at the end of the match was going to be reversing Duchess when she tried to suplex MJ off the top turnbuckle. MJ would land on top of Duchess and pin her, but right before the referee counted to three, Duchess would roll MJ over and pin *her* for the win.

Tika had practiced the suplex and reversal with MJ over and over in one of the rings, with a pile of soft foam mats covering the canvas for them to land on safely.

MJ felt confident in her ability to do the move, and to take the rest of the bumps she was going to take, but the thought of wrestling in front of the crowd again still frightened her.

She took several slow, deep breaths, breathing in through her nose and out through her mouth. MJ found it didn't just help her relax after training, it helped her calm down when she was scared or anxious.

She walked out of the bathroom and nearly ran into Zina, who stood there with her arms folded across her chest.

MJ wasn't sure if Zina was waiting to use the bathroom, or if she was waiting for her.

"I see you ain't setting up chairs anymore," Zina said, and she didn't sound like her usual friendly self.

"Um, Tika wanted to run through some stuff with me for my match."

"Uh-huh."

It was like talking to a stranger. This didn't seem like the same girl MJ had made friends with.

"Are you mad?" MJ asked her.

Zina sighed. "It's just kinda messed up, you know? I've been here a lot longer than you, and I'm not even close to being on the shows yet. Papi says I'm not ready. You're here a couple of *weeks* and just because you and Tika are both Mexican, she picks you to work with her."

MJ felt as though Zina had just punched her in the chest.

"I'm not Mexican," she said. "I'm American."

Zina rolled her eyes. "Whatever."

"It's not whatever!" MJ exploded angrily. "You don't get to tell me what I am! You think it's awesome being Mexican? Did you know the other girls on my gymnastics team wrote 'build the wall' on my locker?"

Instead of backing down, Zina only seemed to get as mad as MJ.

"Look, you don't need to tell me about not being treated like everybody else because of what you are, all right? You ever had someone ask to touch your hair like you're a dog they want to pet? You ever been afraid to laugh too hard at a movie because when you're loud they complain about you to the theater, or even call the cops on you?"

Thinking about Zina experiencing those things hurt MJ way more than any of the words Zina had directed at her. She suddenly remembered what she liked about the older girl—that they both felt like outsiders. No matter how angry MJ was in that moment, she knew that the two of them had more in common than they had differences, despite what they were saying.

She didn't want to fight with Zina, but she didn't know how to stop being mad and tell her that.

Zina seemed to take MJ's silence as MJ not caring about what Zina had just told her.

"You just do you," she said, coldly. "But I see you. Just so you know."

"I didn't ask to be on the shows," MJ insisted. "It just happened."

"Yeah, well, you didn't say 'no' to it, either."

Zina walked away before MJ could respond, not that MJ knew how to explain herself any better than that.

She felt sick. MJ thought she could hear her stomach making noises.

She didn't know how long she'd been standing there lost in her own thoughts when Tika appeared beside her.

"You okay?" she asked, putting her hand on MJ's shoulder.

"I . . . I don't feel so good."

"Are you nervous? You're going to be great!"

MJ stared up at Tika through the holes in her mask. Tika's smile and reassurance usually made her feel better, but right then it somehow made MJ feel worse.

Tika's smile turned into a look of concern. "Are you really sick? Do you want to go home? You don't have to wrestle tonight if you're feeling bad. It's okay."

"No," MJ said, almost automatically.

Then she thought more about it, and she didn't change her mind.

"No," she repeated more firmly. "I want to wrestle."

Tika smiled again and patted her on the back.

"That's more like it," she said. "Now you sound like Chica Relámpago."

As upset as MJ was about her fight with Zina, the thought of letting down the school and disappointing Papi and Tika and the rest of them was worse.

She may not have felt like Lightning Girl, but MJ knew she could act like Lightning Girl.

★ ★ ★ ★ ★ ★ ★ ★ ★ ★

POP

It was the longest match MJ had wrestled so far, and she was breathing so hard and so fast she was afraid she would pass out. MJ didn't know if that was the result of being pushed harder and further in the ring, or her nerves (which were still like a jar full of fireworks), or if it was both.

The crowd did seem bigger that night, and a lot of them appeared to recognize MJ when she'd come out in her Lightning Girl mask.

It surprised her. Deep down MJ didn't believe anybody had really seen the video of her online, and even if they had, Tika certainly couldn't be right about the video bringing more people out to the shows.

Who would pay money to see *her*, after all?

But it looked as though Tika *was* right, and MJ wasn't sure whether that made her feel happy and excited, or sad and terrified.

She still wasn't comfortable or experienced enough to do any complicated holds or slams, and she was too small to believably muscle her opponent around the ring anyway.

MJ was learning the crowd liked it when she jumped around, so that's what she did. Duchess ran at her, and MJ leaped over her head. That was called a leapfrog, and it looked even more impressive because Duchess was so much taller than her. The crowd cheered. MJ turned around and Duchess charged her again, faster this time, and she yelled angrily like MJ was frustrating her. MJ leaped over her a second time, and the crowd in the school cheered even louder.

Their voices went quiet suddenly when Duchess stopped short after running underneath MJ and quickly turned around, clotheslining MJ to the canvas.

The crowd booed as she hit the mat.

The clothesline, and the impact of Duchess's larger body colliding with hers, had actually hurt way more than the bump. MJ didn't think Duchess was trying to be stiff with her. The much more experienced wrestler was just being a good villain.

MJ sucked air through her nose and exhaled through her mouth as Duchess dragged her to her feet.

"Move," she whispered to MJ before she whipped her hard into the turnbuckles.

MJ lay against the corner and waited. She knew that Duchess wanted her to move out of the way when she ran at MJ. Her opponent screamed like she was about to murder the young Lightning Girl, and then Duchess charged, crashing into the turnbuckles as MJ slipped from her path.

MJ, or rather Lighting Girl, had an opportunity to take control of the match. Duchess was curled up against the turnbuckles as if she were really hurt.

The problem was that Duchess hadn't told MJ what to do *after* she moved out of the way.

Nothing was coming into her head. She didn't know what to do.

Fortunately, Tika had given her some advice before MJ went out for the match.

"If you get stuck, and you can't talk to your opponent, just go with what you know."

"What do I know?" MJ had asked her, and even though

it was an honest question, Tika couldn't help laughing.

"Gymnastics," she told MJ. "You're great at gymnastics and you can do tumbles and all that stuff without thinking. That's how we pulled off that big spot at the end of our match. Just throw some flips in there if you get stuck and add a bump at the end. It's a short walk between a gymnastics move and a wrestling move."

With Duchess still waiting and selling that she was hurt, MJ backed all the way into the opposite corner of the ring and charged across the mat at her opponent. As she ran, she performed a cartwheel and then a perfect back handspring flip before letting gravity fling her spine into the other corner.

A loud thrill swept through the crowd as they watched MJ tumble. This time, however, it was Duchess' turn to move out of the way and MJ's turn to crash and burn in the corner.

That didn't matter to MJ, though. She'd heard them react to her flip, and that sound made her feel awesome.

Duchess apparently decided it was time for the finish. She picked up MJ with ease and put her on top of the turnbuckles. Climbing up the corner after her, Duchess hooked her for a suplex and the next thing MJ knew her entire body was pointed upside down ten feet above the canvas as they both fell through the air.

Just as they'd practiced, MJ turned her body with Duchess's help so that she landed on top of the woman when they hit the mat.

MJ was pinning her, and the referee dropped down to his knees to make the count.

The whole crowd seemed to have a single voice in that moment. That giant voice counted eagerly along with each slap of the referee's hand, excited for Lightning Girl to upset Duchess and win the match. People even started rising from their seats and standing in anticipation of the victory.

Just before the three-count, however, Duchess rolled backward and took MJ's body with her, reversing things so that she ended up on top of MJ with MJ's shoulders pinned to the canvas.

This time the referee counted all the way to three, and Duchess was the winner.

The crowd booed louder than MJ had heard them boo at any Saturday night show she'd witnessed.

"Good job, kid," Duchess panted before she climbed off MJ.

MJ had to once again remind herself not to say "thank you" out loud, or even nod, because they weren't supposed to be talking to each other.

The compliment made her happier than she could've explained, anyway.

MJ continued to lie there as Duchess soaked up the jeers of the crowd for a few moments longer. Duchess climbed up the turnbuckles and taunted the people in the front row, drawing even more heat.

After her opponent finally left the ring, MJ slowly got to her feet to do the same.

That's when the strangest thing happened. MJ heard a few people clapping for her, which was nice. A few more people started clapping, and then a few more after that.

Within seconds, the entire audience was applauding her, loudly.

Somewhere beneath that, MJ heard a single voice call out, "Lightning Girl!"

Someone else followed by yelling, "Chica!"

That simple word was repeated by half a dozen other people, and their voices slowly joined together to begin a chant.

"Chi-ca! Chi-ca! Chi-ca!"

The rest of the crowd was quick to join in, and soon everyone was chanting.

"CHI-CA! CHI-CA! CHI-CA!"

It grew so loud that MJ's knees began to shake.

She couldn't believe what was happening. MJ stood

there, with close to two hundred people chanting her name like she was a hero.

She remembered thinking that it was a good thing no one could see her sweat under her mask.

MJ hoped in that moment no one could see her cry under the mask, either.

* * * * * * * * * * *

A LARGER WORLD

MJ couldn't remember when she'd stopped eating her lunch behind the library. It wasn't any kind of conscious decision she'd made. One day, several weeks ago, MJ had simply stopped at the collection of long tables outside the cafeteria instead of walking past them. She did the same thing the next day, and the next, and after a while it just became part of her daily routine.

The first time she'd ever tried to eat at the tables, a group of older kids told her the cafeteria tables were reserved for eighth graders only. MJ knew they weren't telling the truth, but she'd packed away all her things and left the table anyway.

Lucha Dominion was over for the season, but they still

posted short videos exclusively through their app. MJ was watching an interview with Corrina, talking about her victory in the season finale.

MJ still couldn't believe she and Corrina Que Rico were pretty much friends. She smiled as she watched the woman she'd come to know in real life cut a promo totally in character. The Corrina she hung out with at Victory Academy was sweet and nice, so different from the intense persona she used when she was in the ring and on camera.

"So you think you're some kind of wrestler now?"

That voice wasn't coming from the video.

It was Madison.

Who else? MJ thought tiredly.

It was annoying the way Madison always seemed to announce her presence by angrily firing a dumb question at MJ.

The other girls from the gymnastics team surrounded her, as usual.

MJ paused the video she'd been watching and set her tablet down on the table. She looked up at Madison, staring into her eyes.

"What are you talking about?"

"We heard you're going to a wrestling school," Emma explained, sounding far less bothered by it than Madison apparently was.

"That's so cool," Sophia added, drawing a reprimanding look from Madison.

"It is not," she corrected her teammate. "It's probably not even true, anyway."

"I'm just taking some lessons at a school our neighbor runs. He used to be a luchador."

Madison cocked her head to one side like a confused dog. "A what?"

MJ sighed. "Never mind."

"That's so dumb," Madison concluded, even though she obviously had no idea what MJ was talking about. "And fake."

"It feels pretty real when you get knocked down," she told Madison. "And how would you know, anyway? You've never even watched a whole show. You've definitely never been in a wrestling ring."

"Oh, look at you. You really think you're tough now, don't you? It was stupid enough when you just watched that junk all the time. Trying to actually *be* one of them is really making you act like an idiot."

As MJ stared up at Madison, she saw in the other girl's eyes the meanness she always seemed to carry around for no reason. Something occurred to MJ.

She didn't care.

Madison didn't matter to her. None of the other kids

at her school who liked to pick on her mattered, not anymore. She no longer felt nervous or afraid, at least not about going to school and facing other kids.

The world seemed bigger to MJ now, and middle school was just a part of it.

She must've been quiet for too long, because Madison reached for MJ's tablet, no doubt with the intention of taking it away from MJ, or even breaking the device that was a birthday present from her parents.

MJ snatched it away quickly, her eyes narrowing and a fresh, hot spurt of anger rising through her body.

It would feel good to jump up from the table and put Madison in one of the many wrestling holds she'd learned at Victory Academy. A lot of those holds really hurt when you applied pressure. She could take Madison down and make her tap out right there in the middle of the cafeteria tables, in front of everyone.

It was a fun fantasy, but MJ knew she couldn't do that. That's not what Papi had trained her for.

Besides, she didn't really want to do it, either.

Fighting Madison for no reason wasn't worth it.

MJ took a deep breath, the way a wrestler breathed, and when she spoke next she was calm and her voice was even and firm.

"Madison, you can go away, or you can sit down and eat

lunch with me. I don't care either way. But if you touch my stuff or me again, I'm going to have to stop you."

"How are you going to stop me?"

MJ shrugged. "However I need to. And it's not because I'm learning to be a wrestler or I think I'm tough or something. It's because I'm tired of you. You're boring, you're annoying, and I don't want to talk to you anymore."

"Let's just go, Madison," Sophia said.

"Yeah, I wanna eat," Emma seconded.

Madison looked back at them, surprised.

Without the other girls backing her up, Madison seemed to lose a lot of her confidence and menace. She shifted from one foot to the other uncomfortably before staring down at MJ again.

"Don't think I'm afraid of you or anything," Madison warned her.

"I don't think that," MJ said, and she meant it.

Madison seemed satisfied by that, or at least as much as someone so unhappy all the time could be.

They left her alone.

MJ breathed a sigh of relief.

It felt like a small victory, but it was hard for MJ to enjoy that feeling.

She couldn't stop thinking about Zina and the terrible argument they'd had.

MJ used to think she didn't need friends, but lately the friends she'd made at Victory Academy felt every bit as important to her as wrestling had become.

She hoped she could make things right with Zina somehow, but MJ knew it wouldn't be as easy as telling off Madison.

Friends were a lot harder to keep than enemies. That much MJ knew.

* * * * * * * * * *

HARDWAY

Tika was leading class. Mr. Arellano was busy helping Creepshow, who'd brought in a contract he'd been sent for his next tour of Japan. He wanted Papi's help looking it over before he signed it. MJ wasn't exactly sure why, but she knew enough to guess contracts for pro-wrestling jobs were probably complicated things.

There were a dozen students attending class that Saturday afternoon. They were split into two groups, and each group was put in a different training ring. They lined up in rows of three across the canvas.

Usually when they trained, MJ and Zina lined up next to each other, but after the argument they'd had, MJ found herself staring across the warehouse at Zina as they stood in separate rings.

They started out by doing stretches, twisting and bending at their waists, and then sticking out their arms and moving them in little circles. Tika had them all do twenty push-ups on their hands and knees. Through it all, she reminded them to keep breathing.

When everyone was properly loosened up, they all went through bump drills; running in place and taking front bumps, and then back bumps. Tika slowly walked in circles around each ring, calling out to them when she wanted them to bump, and then telling them to stand back up, which they all did as quickly as possible and then started running in place again.

MJ always tried to count the number of bumps they took during drills, but after the first few minutes she never failed to lose her place. It was hard enough just to keep moving and breathing, let alone to keep track of numbers in her head.

"All right, that's enough!" Tika announced, clapping her hands together. "Everybody cool down!"

They all stopped pumping their legs and tried to catch their breath. MJ bent forward and put her hands on her knees.

"Who wants to do some sparring?"

That meant they were about to have a long practice match. Two of them would start out in the ring, and then they could tag in other students to take their place. No one would win and they didn't work out any spots or moves beforehand; they'd just keep wrestling, making it up as they went along, until Tika told them to stop.

"MJ, Zina, you start."

MJ blinked, frozen in place, unsure she'd heard Tika right.

The rest of the students around her climbed through the ropes and stood on the ring apron. The students in the other training ring leaped down and crossed the Academy floor to join them.

MJ was still so surprised that she didn't move. Eventually, Zina rolled into the ring in front of her and stood up to face MJ.

Zina didn't seem to be as shaken as MJ felt, but the other girl also couldn't seem to look directly at MJ. She was sort of staring in her direction without ever meeting MJ's eyes.

"Keep it simple," Tika instructed them. "No big bumps and no high spots. I just want you to work on your flow together."

MJ and Zina circled each other. That part was starting to feel natural to MJ. She was learning most of this was just repetition. You did it over and over again until you didn't even have to think about it, your body and brain did it automatically. She did still have to remind herself to mirror what her opponent was doing as they circled; if Zina turned to one side and moved a foot back, MJ turned the opposite side of her body and moved the opposite foot back.

MJ and Zina locked up and started going through simple holds and reversals. MJ tried to catch Zina's eyes, but Zina still wasn't really looking at her.

After trading holds for a while, Zina grabbed her in a tight headlock. MJ felt pressure around her neck, but it didn't worry her; Zina was simply a lot bigger and stronger than her.

MJ put her arms around Zina's waist, and then pressed her hand against the small of the taller girl's back. She tried to push her, which was supposed to signal to Zina to let go of the headlock, run into the ropes, and bounce back at MJ.

Instead, Zina only tightened her hold.

Confused, MJ tried to shove her off again, this time pushing her harder.

Again, Zina squeezed MJ's head and neck like her arms were snakes choking their food.

Now the headlock was starting to hurt, and MJ knew Zina was doing it on purpose.

Instead of trying to shove her a third time, MJ tried to

shake her head free of Zina's grasp, backpedaling with her feet.

Zina just moved with her, refusing to let go.

Frustrated, angry, and in pain, MJ'd had enough. She wrapped her arms around Zina's waist and, without thinking, lifted her up in the air. With Zina balanced on her shoulder, MJ tossed both of their bodies backward to the mat, dropping Zina with a suplex.

The impact was enough to force Zina to release the hold. MJ rolled away from her and popped back up to her feet.

"I said no big bumps!" Tika yelled at them, but then added, "That looked good, though."

MJ looked down. Zina was still lying there. She didn't look hurt, just surprised by the move.

Having Zina on her back staring up at her made MJ pause. Suddenly she didn't know what to do next. She couldn't think of a move, any move. It was a lot harder when there wasn't a more experienced wrestler telling her what to do, guiding her through the match.

She heard Tika yell, "Don't stop!"

Feeling her nerves rattle and her head buzz, MJ stopped thinking and just reacted. She dropped an elbow down on Zina.

The other girl moved out of the way, however. MJ wasn't

ready for that, and she landed awkwardly on the mat instead of breaking a clean bump.

When MJ stood up again, Zina forearmed her in the chest, hard. She was bigger and stronger than MJ, and the blow not only hurt, it knocked the breath out of her for a second.

MJ thought about hitting her back. A part of her said she *should* hit Zina back. MJ didn't, though. She didn't want to really fight with Zina.

Instead, MJ grabbed Zina's arms and locked up with her, not knowing what else to do. She just wanted to keep Zina from landing another shot.

"Don't lock up again!" Tika shouted at them from outside the ring. "That's like restarting a story in the middle!"

Neither of them moved to untangle themselves at first. Zina finally looked straight into MJ's eyes. There was something that felt so hateful in Zina's stare. It made MJ mad, so she stared hard right back at her.

Zina grabbed MJ's arm and moved to push it away. As she did, her elbow smashed into MJ's nose.

MJ yelped, but more out of surprise than anything. It didn't hurt, not really. There was a weird sensation on impact, like something hard pressing deep into her face. MJ realized it was the bone inside her nose. Then she felt warmth in the middle of her face, and she tasted pennies.

Zina stepped back and MJ touched her nose. *That* stung. She also felt something wet on her fingertips.

The wet stuff was blood.

Her blood.

It was like having a runny nose and not being able to find a tissue. MJ wiped her lips and pressed the back of her wrist just under her nose to stop more blood from leaking out.

"What happened?" Tika asked as she rolled inside the ring and stood up between them.

MJ narrowed her eyes at Zina, shouting at her like an accusation. "She elbowed me in the nose!"

"So?" Zina shot back at her. "It happens."

"Did you do it on purpose?" Tika asked her.

"No," Zina insisted.

Tika repeated the question, her voice unchanged. "Did you do it on purpose?"

This time, Zina didn't answer right away.

"A little," she admitted.

Tika frowned, and Zina looked down at the canvas.

"Hey! Look at me!"

Zina looked up at Tika.

"If you have a problem with another worker and you want to work it out by beating each other up in the ring, that's fine, but you don't try to hurt each other."

"What's the difference?" Zina asked.

"Broken noses," Tika said.

"Her nose isn't broken."

"It could've been. Don't get smart with me. *Student*."

There was no room for argument in the way Tika said that, and Zina didn't try.

It was weird. Watching that, MJ stopped feeling angry and instead felt sorry for Zina. She didn't like seeing Tika yell at her, even if she had popped MJ in the face intentionally.

"I'm not even going to make you apologize, because I don't care if you're sorry. You're not going to do that again. I do want to see you two shake hands, though. Right now."

MJ offered Zina her hand. MJ wasn't even mad about her nose; she just wanted this *thing* between her and Zina to be over. She hated the way it felt, like there was this sharp stick between them, and each end was poking and prodding them both. She just wanted to laugh and feel comfortable with her again. Zina was the first friend MJ made at Victory Academy, and maybe the first friend close to her age she'd made ever. To MJ that had come to mean as much to her as wrestling did.

Zina took her hand. She didn't squeeze it though, and she didn't say anything. The look on her face told MJ shaking hands wasn't fixing anything.

She watched Zina leave the ring without either of them saying a word to each other. MJ sniffed and swallowed hard, raising two fingertips to dab at her face. She tried to make it look like it was her injury that was making her sniffle instead of her feelings.

She turned away and was nearly blinded by a sudden flash of light. She blinked, and when everything faded back into focus, Creepshow was standing there holding a Polaroid camera in one hand and waving the picture he'd just taken of her in his other hand.

"That's totally going on the wall," he announced with a big smile.

MJ flushed. She remembered there was blood all over her face which made her nose hurt more.

She covered her face with her hands. Fortunately, Tika had retrieved a towel from someone and she handed it to MJ.

"Knock it off," Tika chastised Creepshow.

"It's her first hardway!" he protested.

"Hardway?" MJ asked, not recognizing the word.

"It means you got busted open by accident and bled without meaning to," Tika explained.

MJ was even more confused. "When do you *mean* to bleed?"

Creepshow stared at her oddly. "You've seen wrestlers on TV bleed before, right?"

"Yeah, but Papi . . . *my* Papi . . . he . . . he always said the blood in wrestling was fake."

"No disrespect to your papi," Creepshow said, "but he was wrong."

MJ wiped the blood from her chin and mouth and pressed the stained towel under her nose. Doing that still stung a lot worse than actually getting elbowed. She looked past the students on the apron, watching Zina, who'd walked over to the vending machines.

"She'll get over it," Tika assured MJ. "Whatever it is, the heat will fade."

"Did you have us spar on purpose?" MJ asked her.

Tika shrugged. "You two seemed like you needed it."

MJ looked down at the bloody towel in her hand.

"I hope it worked," she said.

Tika laughed, reaching up and gently stroking MJ's arm to console her.

It helped, but only a little.

For something everybody thought was fake, at that moment wrestling felt all too real in more ways than one.

ÁGUILAS Y RATAS

They'd come close to selling out tickets for that night's show and MJ had wrestled in her longest match yet. She went almost a full ten minutes with another, much older student, Marta, who had chosen the gimmick name Tigresa Fuerte. MJ took some of her biggest bumps for Marta, getting bieled out of the corner and across the ring, back body-dropped, and even catching Marta when she dove through the ring ropes and landed on the protective pads outside the ring.

Dives like that were a big part of the lucha libre style of wrestling in particular, and MJ, Tika, and Papi had spent most of the week preparing for her to safely catch her opponent and fall to the floor.

In the end, MJ reversed Marta's attempt at a suplex off the turnbuckles and tossed the older girl over her shoulder and down to the canvas. She held onto Tigresa Fuerte after they hit. Both of them landed with their shoulders on the mat, and the referee counted to three. If Marta's shoulders had stayed down, MJ would have scored the pinfall. Instead, and at the last possible second, Marta lifted one of her shoulders. That meant Marta was now technically pinning MJ, and Tigresa Fuerte was declared the winner.

However, for just a moment the crowd thought MJ had won, and it was the loudest she'd ever heard them cheer.

"I told you she'd get over it," Tika said to Mr. Arellano as MJ walked backstage after the match.

Papi, as usual, appeared totally unimpressed.

He told Tika, "If you break your arm patting yourself on the back you won't be able to work next week."

When the last match was over and everyone in the crowd had filed out of the school, MJ approached Mr. Arellano as she did after each show. In her hands she held her Lightning Girl mask. When she wore the hood, she tried not to think about the fact that it had belonged to Papi's grandson, but MJ always felt a weight pressing down on her because of it.

Before her first match with Tika, Corrina Que Rico had cut a quick and hasty hole in the back of the mask so she could pull MJ's ponytail through it. Since then, some-one had sewn a circle of vinyl the same color as the rest of the mask around that hole to make it look more finished and professional. MJ wasn't sure if Tika had done it, or even Mr. Arellano himself, but it made it feel more like the mask belonged on her head.

Mr. Arellano was barking orders at the new students, most of them even greener than MJ, who were tasked with putting away the chairs and cleaning up the school after shows.

She walked up behind him. "Papi?"

"I'll be ready to take you home in a few minutes," he said without looking at her.

"No, that's not it. I just wanted to give you the mask to put away in your trunk, that's all."

That got his attention. He looked down at her holding the mask without answering her for what felt to MJ like a long time.

"Take it home," he finally instructed her. "Wash it. It smells like cheese someone left out for a week."

"Oh," she said, staring into the mask's empty eyeholes. "Okay. I'll bring it back after school tomorrow."

He waved the idea away. "Just keep it at home. You only need to bring it back for shows."

MJ was surprised to hear him say that.

"Are you sure?"

He nodded. "It's your mask now."

She didn't know what to say to that. She knew what the mask meant, and what a big deal it was for him to give it to her.

Before MJ could think of what to say, Mr. Arellano turned away and started yelling at a teenager who he said was stacking the chairs wrong.

She was sorry the moment was over, but she was also relieved she didn't have to come up with the words to thank him.

MJ hung out and bought a soda from one of the vending machines. She always waited for Mr. Arellano to oversee the breaking down so that he could drive her home. Her mother had yet to come to one of the Saturday night shows. She was taking business classes on the weekends. Her mother said it was so she could get a better job and get them a house like the one they had to leave behind.

After she finished her soda, MJ walked outside, leaving the main door to Victory Academy open so that the sidewalk was bathed in the warehouse's light, and she could still see and hear everyone inside. She'd found that after a show or a hard training session, nothing felt better than walking out into the cool air, feeling it on your skin, and breathing it in deeply.

No one else appeared to be hanging around in front of the school. It was late, and any fans that had lingered after the show to talk to the wrestlers or drink sodas by their cars had all gone home. MJ liked the quiet. It was funny thinking about how before she started attending Victory Academy the quiet at home when she was by herself often got to be too much for her. Now MJ spent so much time around so many people that she was enjoying her alone time again.

A metal rattling sound broke her away from those thoughts and drew her attention. There was an old, rusting ladder bolted to the side of the building that extended all the way to the roof. MJ looked over at the bottom of the ladder and didn't see anything. Then the ladder started shaking.

She jumped back a little bit in alarm and looked up. MJ saw a dark shape moving up the ladder.

"What . . .?" she mouthed silently.

She didn't have time to make out exactly what it was before the shape disappeared over the top of the ladder and onto the roof.

MJ walked over to the first rung, her eyes still scanning the top of the building. She waited, but the figure didn't reappear.

She looked back at the open door to the school. MJ

knew she should probably run back and tell Papi or one of the older students who was still inside. She didn't, though. Maybe it was wrestling on the Saturday night shows, or the way the other wrestlers treated her like an equal instead of a dumb kid. It might also have been that MJ wanted Papi to see she could handle more things on her own.

She leaped and grabbed the first rung, pulling her body up onto the ladder as easily as she scaled the ring ropes. MJ climbed to the top quickly. She had never been afraid of heights, especially after doing gymnastics for so long.

The only light on the rooftop came from the moon hanging full and bright overhead. It was enough for MJ to spot the dark figure, standing over one of the large pipes that fed down into the warehouse. He'd opened the cap that was attached to it.

The man (MJ assumed from the width of his body that he was a man) wore a long, thick leather trench coat and dark gloves. A mask covered his head and face. Those gloved hands were holding onto a thick cardboard box. It looked like he was preparing to tip the top of the box against the opening of the pipe.

It wasn't just a mask he was wearing, MJ noticed; it was a máscara, a lucha hood. The hood was black, and in the light of the moon she could make out the shape of a bird stitched in green over the face and around the mask's eyeholes. MJ thought it looked like an eagle spreading its wings.

"Hey!" MJ yelled at him. "What are you doing up here?"

The figure's hooded head whipped around and the eyes behind that green eagle stared at MJ in surprise.

At that point MJ realized she probably should have come up with a plan before she got his attention.

She was still thinking about that when the man, in a panic, reared back and threw the box in his hands across the roof at MJ.

It was one of those moments when time seems to slow down, when your eyes go wide, and for just an instant you see what's happening in front of you as clearly as if it were a picture someone made larger on a screen.

As that box hung in the middle of the air, MJ saw rats. Big ones. She saw fat, furry bodies with crooked teeth and gnarled tails flying out from inside that box. There must have been half a dozen of them, the four toes on each of their front feet looking to MJ as big and sharp as monster claws as they catapulted in her direction like something from a bad dream.

She threw her arms up in front of her face and turned her head. MJ felt the bristles of their fur and their plump bodies wriggling as they bounced against her skin.

Fortunately, it only lasted for a split second.

Unfortunately, the reason it only lasted for a split second was the large box slamming into her.

MJ fell backward, losing her balance, and suddenly there was nothing solid underneath her feet. In a panic, her brain informed her that she was falling off the roof. The air rushed up around her and MJ closed her eyes and screamed at the top of her lungs without really hearing the sound she made.

Then it all stopped.

She hadn't hit the ground. MJ knew this because she could feel her legs swinging. Her heart was pumping, and she was breathing hard and fast. She slowly opened her eyes and looked up.

Somehow, and MJ didn't even remember doing it, she'd grabbed onto a rung of the ladder and stopped herself.

She was dangling about twelve feet below the edge of the roof. Her heartbeat slowed down a little, and MJ stopped panicking as the knowledge she wasn't falling anymore set in. The bad part, however, was once she stopped panicking because she wasn't falling, MJ started being afraid she was *going* to fall.

Just don't look down, she thought over and over. *Don't look down.*

MJ suddenly became aware of how sweaty and wet her

hands were. She could feel them slipping around the metal of the ladder rung. That caused her heart to start beating fast again.

Just put your feet back on the ladder, she told herself. *That's all you have to do.*

Slowly, MJ began raising one leg to plant her foot on another rung. The toe of her sneaker was just touching metal when a blood-chilling squeak from right above her head stopped her cold.

She looked up and saw one of the rats wriggling down the side of the ladder. Its eyes shined black in the moonlight, and its teeth looked like broken shards of glass.

MJ screamed again, leaning away as her toe slipped and the lower half of her body began swinging from side to side. Thankfully her hands tightened their grip on the ladder rung.

It's gonna bite me, she thought frantically. *It's gonna bite me and I'm gonna fall oh my god oh my god . . .*

The rat's high-pitched squeaking hurt her ears. MJ shut her eyes tightly. She felt tears sting the inside of her eyelids. Her body began to tremble.

Another voice in her head told her that she had to do something, that she wasn't going to just hang there and wait for the rat to chew her up until she fell to the concrete below.

MJ couldn't, though. She couldn't force her arms and legs to take action. She was too afraid.

She was cursing herself for being such a chicken when it occurred to her that the squeaking had stopped.

Opening her eyes and blinking away tears until the world came back into focus, MJ looked up to see the rat's pink tail slithering over the edge of the roof. It had turned and crawled back up the ladder.

Every muscle in MJ's body seemed to relax at once, and the hot fear coursing through her slowly turned into a cold feeling centered in the pit of her gut.

You're okay, she thought. *You're okay.*

Still trembling, MJ pulled her knees up and pushed her feet against one of the lower rungs. Once she felt like her footing was firm, she hugged her arms around the rung she'd been holding onto and clung to the ladder as tightly as she could.

"Maya, stay there!" a familiar voice shouted up at her from below.

Against her better judgment, MJ looked down. She saw Creepshow standing on the sidewalk, several others running out of the school to join him.

She just nodded, looking back at the wall behind the ladder and hugging the metal even tighter.

She knew he was climbing up beneath her because

she felt the vibrations of the ladder. A few moments later Creepshow was sliding his arms around her waist. He felt warm, and that was comforting in a way MJ couldn't explain. The way he smelled also reminded her of her father. That was even more comforting, and her fear started to roll back like water on a beach.

"Just hold onto me, okay? I got you."

MJ finally let go of the rung and threw her arms around his neck. Creepshow climbed back down the ladder and held her securely as he leaped onto the sidewalk.

"Can you stand up?" he asked, still holding her.

MJ nodded against his neck, though her legs still felt shaky.

He lowered her to the concrete and MJ planted her feet solidly on the sidewalk. As Creepshow released her and stepped away, she felt sad. She'd enjoyed him holding her. Thinking that made her feel weird and embarrassed, however, so she banished the thoughts immediately.

"Thank you."

She had to force the words to come out of her mouth. Her throat felt dry and ragged.

"What's going on out here?" Mr. Arellano shouted, pushing his way through the bodies that had gathered around MJ.

"She was hanging off the ladder," Creepshow explained,

pointing up at the rooftop. "I had to go up and get her."

"The ladder? What were you doing up there?" Mr. Arellano demanded.

"Rats," MJ stammered. "Rats . . . masked man . . . dumping rats . . . threw them at me . . ."

The old man shook his head. "What are you babbling about, girl?"

"There was someone up on the roof with rats!" she blurted out.

Papi frowned deeply, but he wasn't as disturbed by the news as she would have expected him to be.

"We've had to chase dumb kids off that roof before," he explained. "I don't know why they like farting around up there so much. Now they're putting *other* people in danger, not just themselves."

MJ was already shaking her head, but before she could protest or suggest he might be wrong, Mr. Arellano seemed to have already moved on.

"We better not have rats *again*," he was saying to his nephew.

"Let's just get her inside, Tío," Creepshow told him.

Creepshow put his arm around her shoulders and gently guided her toward the main entrance to the school.

MJ walked with him, glad to be so close to him again, but not allowing her brain to think about it too much.

Instead, she asked herself a question: *Why would anyone want to dump a box of rats into the school?*

Whatever Papi thought, it didn't feel to her like kids playing a prank or horsing around where they weren't supposed to be. The person she saw up there didn't look like a kid, either, even a really big one. It was more like something from a bad wrestling storyline, only this was real.

It was real enough to almost kill her.

* * * * * * * * * *

HOME VISIT

The Epsom salt always smelled like dishwashing deter-gent to MJ, and she had to pinch her nose closed as she poured it into the water filling the bathtub.

Her elbows were sore from hitting the ring floor, and the rest of her body ached from taking so many bumps throughout the week. She stood in the bathroom wearing an oversized T-shirt that had belonged to her father and might as well have been a dress on her. She was turning the bathwater into a cloudy mess with the chemical salt that would make her muscles feel better after they soaked in it for a while.

It wasn't her first Epsom salt bath. She used to take them all the time when she did gymnastics, especially after competitions. That was one of the few easy parts of dealing with her mother when it came to MJ training at Victory Academy; her mother was used to MJ being sore and needing to soothe minor injuries from gymnastics, so she didn't freak out when MJ came home from the wrestling school with a few aching body parts.

Steam rose from the hot water in the tub. MJ was excited about sinking into the bath, despite the smell. She turned away from the mirror and began lifting her shirt. MJ hated the mirror in the bathroom of the house they were renting. It covered practically the whole wall above the sink and counter. That made it impossible to avoid. The mirror in their old bathroom was a smaller round thing that didn't follow her around the room.

MJ stopped when she heard her mother's voice yelling at her from the living room.

"Maya! Can you come out here, please?"

She didn't sound mad, at least. MJ made sure the knob that controlled the water was turned off tightly before walking out of the bathroom and down the hall.

What she saw when she turned the corner stopped her cold. Neal Corto was standing in their living room. She recognized him right away. He might have even been wearing the same cheap-looking, badly fitted suit he wore when MJ first saw him at Victory Academy.

He was smiling in the same fake way he'd smiled at Mr. Arellano while writing him tickets.

"This is Mr. Corto," her mother explained. "He's from the State Athletic Commission."

"I know who he is," MJ said, and she didn't even try to sound happy about it.

Her mother's eyes flashed angrily at her. "Maya Jocelyn Medina, don't be rude."

"I'm sorry," MJ said automatically. "Hello, Mr. Corto."

Corto seemed unruffled by the icy greeting. He was smiling the whole time.

"It's nice to see you again, Maya," he said. "You look healthy. I'm glad you're okay."

MJ's eyebrows crinkled in confusion.

"What do you mean?"

Instead of answering her, Corto looked at her mother. The smile left his face, and his expression turned serious.

"Mrs. Medina, we've received a report that there was an incident involving Maya here at Victory Academy a few evenings ago."

MJ's mother immediately looked at her as if she expected MJ to explain.

"The incident also involved a ladder," Corto added.

MJ's eyes widened. She hadn't expected him to know about that. She wondered if someone had told him. Would anybody from the school betray the rest of them like that?

She quickly told that thought to go away. MJ decided he must've overheard the other students talking about it while he was doing one of his weekly inspections.

"Maya?" her mother asked, waiting, and not at all patiently.

"I . . . after the show on Saturday, I saw someone shady climbing up a ladder outside the school, so I went up to see what they were doing, and I slipped. But just for a second. I didn't get hurt."

MJ wasn't sure why she left out the part about the hooded man throwing a box of live rats at her. Perhaps she thought that detail would only make what happened worse in her mother's eyes, and this was already a bad situation.

"Why didn't you tell me?" her mother demanded.

"I was fine! Nothing happened!"

"You fell off a roof!"

"I didn't fall!"

"What were you doing outside downtown by yourself?"

"I was just cooling off in the air! I was standing right by the door!"

"So you were unsupervised at the time?" Corto asked her, having been standing there patiently while she and her mother yelled back and forth.

That question hit MJ harder than most of her

opponents in the ring. She knew that was a serious accusation coming from Corto, and her answer could be damaging to the school.

"I . . . it wasn't like that! I just climbed up a ladder and slipped. That's all. It was over in two seconds."

"You should know better," her mother said. "And someone should've been watching you."

Now MJ was angry. "I'm not a baby! They don't treat me like one there. They treat me like a wrestler!"

"You're *not* a wrestler," her mother reminded her. "You're a student."

"I'm sorry if I've upset you, Mrs. Medina," Corto said.

MJ hated how concerned and polite he was being. She'd seen the way he treated Mr. Arellano, and she knew he was exactly like teachers at her school who always acted nice when parents were around, but who were always nasty to kids like MJ.

"It was my duty to investigate, and to inform you," Corto continued. "It's not Maya's fault. She's just a child. The fault lies with the staff at that warehouse and the environment and culture they create."

"It's not a warehouse, it's a school," MJ grumbled.

"You watch yourself, young lady," her mother warned. "You're in enough trouble."

"I won't bother you further right now," Corto said.

"Thank you for your time."

"Thank you for taking the time to let me know what's going on. I'm embarrassed to say I needed it."

"Oh, don't be embarrassed. We all need a little help sometimes. For the good of our kids."

You're so full of it, MJ thought. She desperately wanted to say it out loud but didn't dare.

"Good evening, Mrs. Medina."

"To you too, Mr. Corto."

"Goodbye, Maya," Corto said to her.

MJ didn't answer him. She didn't want to give him the satisfaction.

"Maya Jocelyn," her mother began sternly. "If I have to tell you one more—"

"Goodbye," MJ said through clenched teeth.

Corto left their house. MJ could barely contain herself until the door had snapped closed behind him.

"He's twisting things all around, Mom!" she exploded. "He comes to the school every week to write tickets for things he makes up because he hates wrestling and Mr. Arellano. Everybody at the school says so!"

"If he's citing Mr. Arellano for violations, I'm sure it's for things that are wrong at the school."

"Just because he's an adult and wears a suit doesn't mean he's right and I'm wrong. You just met him five minutes ago. Why won't you listen to me?"

"Because I know how much you love wrestling and love going to that school, and I know you're not thinking clearly when it comes to the subject of both."

"I love it because it's a good place."

"Maya . . . this is all too much. You were supposed to be taking a few lessons every week at a school. You weren't supposed to be fighting on wrestling shows and almost falling off roofs."

"I *didn't* fall!" MJ insisted.

"It doesn't matter!" her mother shouted, louder and angrier than before.

MJ knew better than to say anything else right then.

Her mother sighed deeply. All the anger seemed to flow out of her. MJ thought she just looked sad and tired, and it made her feel bad, like those feelings were MJ's fault.

"I blame myself for a lot of this," her mother said quietly. "I've been so focused on work and school and trying to deal with everything that's happened to us that I haven't been paying attention to you like I should. I think after all our arguing about it, I was almost happy about Victory Academy because it gave you somewhere to go and something to do while I was working late and taking classes. And that's me being a bad mom."

"You're not a bad mom," MJ assured her, and she meant

it. "You take care of us. You take care of me. I know I don't always make it easy on you. It's not on purpose."

"I know that, baby. We're both doing the best we can, but you're a kid. You get some room to mess up. I'm the adult. I don't have that luxury."

"You didn't mess up. Really. Wrestling has been helping me, Mom. A lot. It really has."

"You've been happier lately," her mother admitted. "It's good to see. You have no idea. But I can't let you get away with things all the time. That's not fair to either of us."

"Please don't make me stop going to the school," MJ pleaded. "This wasn't because of wrestling or Mr. Arellano. I just did a dumb thing. I won't do it again. I swear."

Her mother rubbed her temple as if she had a headache, but she didn't speak.

"Mr. Arellano yelled at me too," MJ said. "About the ladder. And he didn't tell me not to tell you. I did that. It's my fault."

Her mother thought about it for a while longer.

MJ waited, her heart feeling like it was trying to break through her chest.

"All right," she announced, as if she'd reached a decision. "No training and no show next week. That's your punishment."

MJ nodded right away. That was nothing compared to

the idea of never being allowed to go back to the school.

"I'd ground you outright," her mother said, "but you don't go anywhere else anyway."

"I go to school."

"Well, you're not getting out of that."

They shared a laugh over that. It was a quiet laugh, and it didn't last long, but it seemed to help them both feel a little better.

"Go soak," her mother instructed her. "Your bath is getting cold."

"Thank you, Mom. I really am sorry, and not just because you found out."

"Thanks for saying that. I appreciate it. No more not telling me things, Maya. Okay?"

"I promise."

MJ meant what she said; she just hoped nothing else would happen that she wouldn't want to tell her mother about.

★ ★ ★ ★ ★ ★ ★ ★ ★ ★ ★

CANCELED SHOW

"Everybody quiet!" Papi yelled. "¡Cállanse!"

The half-dozen conversations happening behind the curtain at Victory Academy all stopped at the same time. The student and professional wrestlers filling the backstage area turned their eyes to Mr. Arellano and his clipboard containing that evening's card scribbled in Papi's barely readable handwriting.

MJ was sitting next to Tika, happy to be back after missing the last show, and the two of them had been talking about how awesome Corrina's last match of the season was against Doña Inez on Lucha Dominion.

"You can hear them out there, right?" Mr. Arellano asked the room, not really expecting an answer.

They all could. The sound of the people on the other side of the curtain, all of them having paid to attend the Saturday night show, was far louder than usual. The first match hadn't even started yet, but the crowd already sounded excited to be there.

"There are over three hundred people out there," he told them. "It's been standing room only for the last hour. It's the biggest crowd we've ever had for a regular Saturday show that wasn't a special event, like our anniversary cards."

Tika gently jabbed MJ with her elbow, grinning down at her.

MJ just shifted in her chair uncomfortably. She knew Tika was trying to give her credit, and MJ appreciated that, but she still didn't like being the center of attention, or how some others in the school were reacting to it.

"I want to tell you all something," Papi continued. "One video on the internet doesn't do that. You hear? The best that does is getting a few extra people in the building once. They stay, and they keep coming back, because of the whole show. You all did that, and I'm proud of each of you, whether you're green as baby caca, or you're a pro who comes back and does these shows to pay it forward to the school and help the students. ¿Entienden?"

He didn't look at MJ as he said all of that, but she knew some of it was aimed at her. She wasn't sure how to feel about that. He didn't sound angry with her anymore, and MJ agreed that everyone on the card should get credit for how popular their little school shows were lately.

"It's a packed house," Papi reminded them. "Let's make it worth their time. What do you say?"

Everyone clapped and yelled out their enthusiasm and their eagerness to put on an amazing wrestling show.

Tika leaned in close and whispered to MJ, "He's right, but don't forget how much you've done to help the school. You hear me?"

MJ tried to silently agree with her by nodding, but Tika wouldn't have it.

"Don't give me that shy stuff, girl. I want to hear you say it."

MJ's cheeks flushed.

"I know," she said.

Tika nodded, satisfied. "That's better."

MJ was nervous, as nervous as she'd been before her first match with Tika. Earlier in the week, Papi told her she was ready to start getting in some offense, which meant that instead of just taking big bumps in her matches, MJ was actually going to get to do some moves on her opponent.

The announcement about the crowd only hammered her nerves further.

She still wasn't going to win, of course, but just the idea that she was going to be responsible to perform moves instead of taking them was enough to scare her. Tika had worked with her throughout the week on a few offensive maneuvers, helping her practice each over and over again. MJ learned how to execute a flying leg-scissors takeover, throw a dropkick, and perform a flying body splash. She was planning to string all of them together in one sequence in her match.

She was picturing in her head how each part of that sequence should look when Neal Corto slipped through the curtain in front of her, clutching a cheap-looking briefcase.

MJ's concentration was shattered by the sight of the weaselly man and the open hatred for Victory Academy that dripped from his every look and gesture.

She wasn't the only one whose attention was pulled away from what they'd been doing by Corto's sudden appearance. Mr. Arellano handed off his clipboard to Tika as soon as he spotted the smaller man and walked over to him.

"The audience isn't allowed back here," Papi said.

Corto grinned. "I'm here on official business."

The backstage area fell quiet again. Everyone was watching the exchange now.

"Well, we're pretty busy tonight, as you can see. What can I do for you, Neal?"

"Bad news, Álvaro," Corto began, and the way he sounded so satisfied made MJ immediately afraid. "There's not going to be any show tonight."

MJ felt her mouth fall open. She looked around at the others, and they seemed just as confused as she was in that moment.

Mr. Arellano sighed. "You can't stop the show, no matter how many little rule violations you find."

"Or make up," Tika added, coughing over her words.

Everyone laughed at that.

MJ looked at Corto, expecting the laughter to make him mad. He didn't look angry, though.

In fact, he looked happier than she'd ever seen him.

Corto shook his head. "I'm afraid I'm not here to write you up for minor infractions."

"Then what do you want?" Mr. Arellano demanded.

In answer, Corto opened his briefcase and pulled out a sheaf of multicolored pieces of paper. He presented them to Papi with that same sour grin on his face.

"This is a notice that your license has been temporarily suspended," he informed the old man, politely. "Pending a review by the athletic commission. Until then, no more shows, no more classes, no more Victory Academy. And I'm sorry to tell you, I expect at that hearing the decision to pull your license will become permanent."

MJ was struck speechless by the proclamation, but everyone else around her started voicing their shock, anger, and protest right away.

"Quiet!" Mr. Arellano ordered.

As the protests died down, he stared hard at Corto. When Papi spoke, his voice was unusually quiet. He didn't even sound mad.

"How did you finally convince them to suspend my license after all these years?"

"Child endangerment," Corto explained. "Creating an unsafe environment for minors. Like her."

He pointed directly at MJ.

Her eyes widened in surprise and alarm.

"It's time you realize you can't pull kids off the streets and teach them to fall on their faces just so you can line your pockets. She should be playing softball or something, not getting beat up by people twice her size."

MJ wanted to speak up, to tell Corto that wasn't true. Mr. Arellano hadn't pulled her off the street, and she knew he cared about her, and about all his students and wrestlers.

She just couldn't make any words come out of her mouth.

Mr. Arellano reached up and silently took the papers from Corto's hand.

"At a loss for words, Álvaro?" he asked the old man. "That's a first."

Papi still didn't say anything. He never looked away from Corto, staring into the younger man's eyes the whole time, but Mr. Arellano didn't say another word. There was no real expression on his face. It appeared empty.

That seemed to please Corto more than anything else.

"I'll see you at the hearing, okay?" he said, then turned around and slipped back through the curtain like the snake he was.

No one spoke, not for a long time.

Mr. Arellano stared down at the official forms in his hands, reading each line carefully.

He still had that blank look on his face.

"Papi?" Tika finally said, unsure what to do.

"Mo!" Mr. Arellano called to their ring announcer, who quickly jogged over in his tuxedo.

"What do you want to do?" he asked.

"Send everyone home. The show is over."

★ ★ ★ ★ ★ ★ ★ ★ ★ ★

WEEKEND VISIT

"**Y**ou're doing the right thing," her mother assured her. "You'll feel better after this, I promise."

MJ wasn't really listening to her. She was staring out through the car window, watching the world zip past without really seeing any of it. She was trying to think of anything else besides where they were going and why and what she had to do when they got there.

It had felt right to her that morning, probably because she was so freaked out about the Saturday show getting canceled, and so worried about what was going to happen with the school. Going with Mom to visit Papi finally felt like something she wanted to do, instead of something MJ was being forced to do. Victory Academy had become a way to escape, to escape everything, but now she needed an escape from her fear of losing the school and wrestling and all the people she'd come to know there.

That feeling of rightness was fading with every mile they drove. It was being replaced by the familiar knots in her stomach, the same painful tightness that had happened there when she'd tried to make this trip with her mother before.

It always looked like a park at first, and MJ liked parks, so she could almost make herself believe everything was going to be fine. As their car moved slowly through the black iron gates, however, she started to see the headstones. There were hundreds and probably more, some little and some big, but all of them were there for the same reason; they marked where a person was buried in the cemetery.

Papi had died on a Tuesday, just a regular Tuesday like the hundreds and thousands of Tuesdays that came before. Her parents were upstairs in their old house, and MJ heard her mother yelling. At first she thought Mom was mad at Papi, and they were having a fight. It didn't take long for MJ to realize her mother wasn't mad, she was scared.

When MJ tried to go into their bedroom, her mother ordered her to stay out. When the ambulance came, her mother held her back so she never really saw Papi's face as they wheeled him out of that room, two big paramedics in their uniforms trying to save his life after his heart had stopped beating for no reason MJ ever came to understand. She still remembered the flashing lights of the ambulance as they followed it to the hospital in her mother's car. MJ couldn't believe Papi was inside of it.

She never saw her father again, first because her mother wouldn't let her, and then later at the hospital, because MJ didn't want to see him. The doctor asked them, but she just couldn't. If she didn't see him like that, then he couldn't be dead, or at least that was what she told herself at the time.

MJ barely remembered the hospital, but she remembered the cemetery. She remembered their whole family gathered here, both sides, Mom's family barely talking to Papi's and Papi's family ignoring them right back, like they were at two different funerals. She remembered her abuelita, Papi's mother, crying without making a single sound. She remembered the uncomfortable dress she wore that her mother picked out and MJ absolutely hated.

There was nothing about that day that wasn't awful, and the worst of it happened in this place, where her papi was buried and would remain forever.

Their car slowed down, and her mother parked

alongside the curb of the road that seemed to wind end-lessly through the inside of the cemetery.

MJ was reminding herself over and over again about how she wanted to tell Papi about the wrestling school, and what was happening, and everything she was afraid of losing.

There was one problem, though. MJ wanted to tell him about all of those things so he could reassure her, so he could make it all okay like he used to.

He couldn't do that for her anymore, and she knew it.

"Are you ready?" Mom asked.

MJ nodded, reaching up and grabbing the handle of the car door.

Her hand just stayed there, holding onto that handle and not moving.

She felt like she couldn't breathe, but she *was* breathing, fast and hard.

"I can't," MJ said, and it was barely a whisper.

"What, baby?" her mother asked, not able to hear her.

"I can't do it!" she said, louder and much angrier.

MJ wasn't mad at Mom for making her repeat the words, she was mad at herself for saying them.

Her mother didn't say anything back at first. Maybe she was waiting to see if her daughter would calm down and change her mind, MJ didn't know, but the silence only made it worse.

"Are you sure, Maya?" she asked, doing that thing MJ hated where she asked a question and obviously wanted a specific answer.

MJ shook her head really fast, not wanting to speak anymore. It was somehow less painful if she didn't have to admit it.

"Okay, sweetheart. It's okay. We'll try again another time."

Her mother was trying not to sound like it, but she was disappointed, MJ was certain. It wasn't the first time they'd had this conversation, just as it wasn't the first time they'd driven back to the cemetery to visit Papi only for MJ to not be able to get out of the car.

She stayed quiet while her mother turned them around and drove them back out through the gates.

The farther away they got, the more MJ's heart slowed down and her brain stopped fizzing and her stomach untied itself.

"I'm sorry I broke our deal," she muttered a few minutes later, remembering the promise she'd made that if Mom allowed her to train at Victory Academy, MJ would finally make this visit.

"Don't worry about that," her mother insisted. "I told you, this isn't part of that. You'll visit Papi when you're ready."

MJ couldn't tell her mother that she'd never be ready, but it felt like the truth.

* * * * * * * * * *

CUTTING PROMOS

The place in which the hearing was to be held was nothing like MJ had imagined. It was a small, stuffy, windowless room with rectangular lights in the ceiling that hurt MJ's eyes.

In fact, the whole building was completely different than she thought it would be. She had pictured some kind of great big carved stone structure that looked old, like city hall or a grand courthouse. Instead, the State Athletic Commission was housed in a one-story fiberglass building that looked like an ugly box from the outside.

The athletic commission was composed of three members, a man and a woman who looked to be Mr. Arellano's age, and a younger man. He reminded MJ of her father, at least a little. They all wore suits and had papers and yellow folders stacked in front of them on a folding wooden table that was, MJ noted, very much like the tables used in wrestling shows.

There were rows of uncomfortable plastic chairs lined up that faced the table. MJ was sandwiched between Mr. Arellano and her mother as they filed into one of the rows to sit down. Tika and about a half-dozen other students from Victory Academy were with them, including Zina, who still wasn't speaking to MJ.

Creepshow had gone back to Japan for a two-week tour and Corrina was away shooting the next season of Lucha Dominion that evening, so neither of them could be there.

MJ spotted Corto as they sat. He was leaning against the corner behind the commission's table, his arms folded across his chest as he surveyed the group from the school with a smug smile on his face.

Mr. Arellano noticed him too. MJ heard the old man mutter a Spanish curse word she didn't recognize.

"Who are the other people, Papi?" she asked.

"The younger one in the middle is Commissioner Lopez," he whispered back to her. "He's in charge. I forget the other two's names, but they all get a vote in what happens to us."

MJ nodded.

"This isn't like, a real courtroom or anything, right?" her mother asked Mr. Arellano. "Maya doesn't have to talk to them if she doesn't want to?"

"I want to, Mom!" MJ insisted.

Her mother had been disturbed by the charges the commission was leveling against Mr. Arellano and the school. It had taken a long time to convince her Corto was an angry little bureaucrat with a grudge who hated wrestling and hated the old man and his school. Even then, she wasn't happy about the situation, and had only agreed to bring MJ to the hearing because she saw how upset the whole thing had made her daughter.

"She doesn't have to do anything," Mr. Arellano assured her. "You two don't even have to be here."

"I *want* to be here, and I'm *going* to talk to them," MJ repeated, feeling ignored and hating it.

"Watch your tone, young lady," her mother reprimanded her.

"Listen to your mamá," Mr. Arellano added.

"Sorry," MJ grumbled.

"Are we ready to get started?" Commissioner Lopez asked loudly, addressing the whole room.

No one answered him, but everyone's attention was firmly on him and the other commission members at that moment.

"Okay then," he said.

MJ wasn't sure what to think about him yet. The commissioner didn't strike her as a mean man, at least right away. He seemed polite, actually. She hoped she was right about that.

Commissioner Lopez read off a paper in front of him.

"We've convened today to rule on the status of Álvaro Arellano's license to promote professional wrestling in the state of California. Mr. Arellano, you own and operate a professional wrestling school called Victory Academy, where you also promote weekly shows."

Papi stood up to address the commission members.

"I do," he confirmed, proudly.

"Thank you. And several of your students, who also perform on your shows, are under the age of eighteen?"

"They are. My youngest student is twelve, I believe."

"And they all participate in these events with the knowledge and consent of their parents?"

"Of course, sir. Every student not of legal age has to have their parent or guardian sign a waiver before they can train at Victory Academy."

"As I'm sure you know, Mr. Arellano, the California State Athletic Commission currently has no guidelines that list a minimum age for students at a pro-wrestling school.

However, I take the charges against you and your school very seriously."

Mr. Arellano nodded gravely. "As you should. I do, too, I promise you."

"We have a report from one of our field investigators that alleges you are creating an unsafe environment for minor children. You're engaging them in dangerous practices, and you're doing it unsafely. These practices have caused injuries that could potentially be very severe, even lethal."

"I understand."

"And what do you say to all of that?"

Papi took a deep breath. "Wrestling is dangerous," he answered, thoughtfully. "Like football. Like any sport or physical activity kids participate in."

"But in those other activities no one is getting hit in the head with chairs or set on fire," the older woman sitting next to Commissioner Lopez said.

She didn't sound to MJ like a wrestling fan.

"I don't teach my students to hit people with chairs or set anyone on fire," Mr. Arellano told her, keeping his tone calm and even. "I teach them how to wrestle and how to protect themselves and their fellow wrestlers in the ring. I'm a second-generation luchador. Lucha, or any kind of professional wrestling, isn't about hurting people or getting hurt. It's about entertaining people and telling them a story. Wrestlers work together to do that. They're not out there to hurt each other. It's like a dance. That's what I teach."

"Thank you for clarifying that, Mr. Arellano," the commissioner said, and he sounded sincere. "I do have to ask, however, how often injuries occur in that teaching, and if you're doing everything you can to minimize that risk."

"Commissioner Lopez, I can stand here all day and tell you that my school is a safe place for kids of any age to come and learn the craft, the art form of lucha libre. I can also tell you how important it is, particularly to Hispanic children, to learn about the culture and heritage that lucha represents for them. But I think it's more important you hear from the person who these charges, and the future of Victory Academy, affects the most, and that's my youngest student, Maya here."

Commissioner Lopez looked a little surprised by that, but he also seemed to be interested in the idea of talking to MJ.

"I think that would help us immensely," he said. "I'd love to hear from her."

Mr. Arellano looked down at MJ and nodded to her, and she knew it was her turn.

Before she stood up, her mother squeezed MJ's knee and smiled at her. It was a nervous smile, and MJ could tell her mother still didn't want to be here. She smiled back just the same, trying to let her mother know it was okay and that she wasn't scared.

She was, of course. MJ was terrified as she stood up and saw the three members of the commission staring across the room at her expectantly. She had a sudden and panicked fantasy about running out of the room, all of them watching her in disbelief.

Instead, MJ closed her eyes. She tried to remember the last time she was standing in the middle of a big crowd of people like this in a strange place.

What she saw behind her eyes, lighting up the darkness there, was her father. The two of them were in the stands of an arena, watching a live taping of an episode of Lucha Dominion. He'd taken her to one for her birthday after the first season of the show had premiered and they'd both fallen in love with it.

MJ had never been to a wrestling show before. It was big and loud and hot and crowded, with everyone around them shouting and jumping as they tried to navigate their way through the chaos. She'd felt so small, like she'd get swallowed up by all the thrashing bodies around her. People were bumping into her and she couldn't see anything.

Just when she was ready to run away from it all, the same way she wanted to run out of the conference room now, her father had touched her hair. MJ had looked up at him then, and he smiled in a way that told her everything would be all right.

MJ remembered how safe she felt in that moment, just knowing he was there. She *knew* nothing bad could happen to her, not while he was around. They found their seats together and ate hot dogs and drank sodas and watched their favorite wrestlers and luchadores, laughing and cheering along with everyone else, her papi just as excited as she was whenever someone dove out of the ring onto their opponent. She loved seeing him like that, happy, like wrestling made him a little kid again.

It was one of the best nights of her life.

When MJ opened her eyes she felt calmer. She breathed in through her nose and out through her mouth, the way Mr. Arellano and Tika had showed her to breathe when she was in the ring working a match.

"Hello," she began, the word sticking a little.

She cleared her throat and continued, speaking louder. "My name is Maya Jocelyn Medina, and I'm twelve years old. This year I started sixth grade at Cesar Chavez Middle School, and I started training at Victory Academy with Mr. Arellano."

"Thank you for coming here to talk to us today, Maya," Commissioner Lopez said.

"You're welcome."

"Maya," Commissioner Lopez said, "have you gotten hurt learning to wrestle at Mr. Arellano's school?"

"Yes," she said, because it was the truth.

He nodded. "Can you tell me how?"

"I . . . have bruises on my elbows because I keep hitting them on the mat when I slap out. Tika says I'm awkward with my arms, but I'm getting better about it. I'm sore the next morning after training a lot. We do a lot of drills, the same thing over and over."

"Is that all?"

"Yes."

MJ fell silent, then she added, quickly, "I've gotten hurt worse doing gymnastics."

Commissioner Lopez actually laughed at that, just a little. "Okay. Do you ever feel like Mr. Arellano or anyone else at the school pushes you too hard? Do they want you to keep drilling and training even when you're hurt?"

MJ shook her head. "They're not like that. Tika's my friend. She would never do anything that would get me hurt."

"I see. Okay. And can you tell me a little bit about what you learn at the school?"

"Like Papi . . . Mr. Arellano . . . said. I learn to wrestle. I couldn't even get inside the ring until they said I was ready. I started on mats on the floor, just learning holds and reversals. After that, mostly I've been learning how to bump. You have to know how to land right when you fall in the ring, or you *will* get hurt."

"I hear you. And you've actually had wrestling matches on the shows at the school, in front of people?"

MJ nodded. "Yes. A few."

"Is that usual? For a twelve-year-old to be in a wrestling match against grown-ups?"

"No. I wasn't supposed to be on the shows yet, but somebody got hurt one night. Tika needed an opponent. It was only supposed to be the one match, but we did a move that people really liked, and a bunch of people posted videos of it, so they've been letting me do that one spot on every show. Papi needs the money . . . because of all the fines Mr. Corto makes him pay every week."

She didn't look over at Corto, and that was on purpose. MJ didn't want to see how he reacted to what she'd just said. She thought she could feel his eyes burning into her, however.

"All right, thank you again, Maya," Commissioner Lopez said, sounding like they were done.

"Can I say something else?" she asked quickly.

"Of course," the commissioner encouraged her. "Please tell us anything you'd like us to know."

MJ took a deep breath. "I . . . things have been . . . or they were . . . bad. Or hard, I guess, especially this last year. My papi . . . my father . . . he . . . he's not around anymore."

She closed her eyes for just a moment. MJ wasn't ready to talk about his death, not in front of a room full of strangers, or maybe the thought of admitting out loud to them all that he was gone would be too much, and she wouldn't be able to get through the rest.

"We moved, my mom and me. I don't have a lot of friends at school. I don't have any friends at school, to tell you the truth. I stopped doing gymnastics because the other girls . . . they didn't want me there. I don't know why, really. I try. I really try. I've just never been good at . . . talking to people, especially the way I wish I could talk to them. So they think I'm weird, I feel like. I don't know why they have to be so mean all the time, even if they don't like me, but that's the reason, I guess."

MJ was quiet for a moment. She hadn't planned to tell them all of that. It just came out. She felt everyone watching her, and it was like a giant, hot light was shining down right on her.

Still, she had to tell them the rest. It was for the school.

"Anyway. What I'm trying to say is, I didn't have

anywhere outside of my house to go. I didn't have anybody . . . my mom's great, she's always there for me, but she doesn't like most of the stuff I like, you know? I got so tired and sick of feeling alone all the time. Then I met Mr. Arellano. He didn't even want to train me. He said I was too young. But I wouldn't stop bugging him."

The group from Victory Academy laughed at that, and MJ noticed that Commissioner Lopez smiled, too.

"I feel good when I'm at Victory Academy. I feel happy again. I know I'm welcome there. That's like, a big deal. To know they want me to be there, and that I don't have to ask to hang out or be part of things. I just know I'm included. And I love wrestling. I've always loved wrestling, ever since I first watched it with my papi. He . . . he loved it too. I didn't think I could be a wrestler. Mr. Arellano and everyone else, they're helping me do things I never even imagined I could do. I love it there. It's my favorite place in the world right now."

The room was quiet after she finished, and MJ wished someone would say something. They were all still looking at her. Mr. Arellano had a strange expression on his face, one MJ didn't remember seeing before. Her mother was actually crying a little, and that made MJ frown because she felt guilty.

"Thank you very much, Maya," the commissioner said.

"I really appreciate you being so honest with us. You can sit down now."

"You're welcome," MJ said again.

She lowered her body into the plastic chair. She did it slowly and carefully, because her legs felt weak right then.

"All right, I think we've heard enough," Commissioner Lopez announced to them all. "We'll recess for a few minutes to discuss everything you've said, and then we'll give you our decision."

MJ watched as the three of them behind the table stood up and shuffled out of the room through a side door.

Corto followed close behind them, and MJ noticed he looked far less satisfied and smug than he had when they first sat down.

Her mother slid an arm around MJ's shoulders and hugged her too tightly.

"You did *so* good," she whispered, sniffling from the tears she'd cried during MJ's speech. "I'm so proud of you."

"Mom, stop!" MJ whispered. "You're embarrassing me."

"I am not!" she insisted, but she did let go of MJ.

Tika leaned around Mr. Arellano to say with a smile, "You killed that, girl!"

"Thanks, Tika."

The only one who didn't congratulate her right away was Papi. Mr. Arellano didn't even look at her, in fact.

He stared straight ahead for a long time with that strange expression on his face.

MJ didn't know what to think. She was starting to wonder if everyone else was wrong, and she'd done a bad job, somehow, telling her story to the commission.

Finally, Mr. Arellano leaned down just enough to speak into her ear.

"Whatever happens, that was a heck of a promo you just cut," he told her.

MJ felt her chest swell, and she smiled.

"Thank you, Papi."

It was another five minutes before the commission, led by Lopez, reentered the room and sat back down behind their table.

At first, MJ didn't see Corto. He wasn't following on their heels like he had been when the commission walked out.

When Corto did walk through the door, his head was hung low so that MJ couldn't see his face, and he strode quickly back to his corner.

"Everyone on this panel has children," the commissioner began. "I have a daughter around your age, Maya. And I think it's safe to say that at one point and on some level or another, we've all watched our children face some truly tough times, much tougher than kids should have to face. It seems to me that these days kids are exposed to so much more than we were when we were your age. You can't even feel safe in your own schools with the world the way it is."

MJ wasn't sure what to make of those words.

"It also seems like kids these days need all the help they can get. They need as many safe spaces as they can find. And it certainly seems to me like you've found one at Victory Academy, Maya."

MJ felt all the air leave her body, but in a good way. She realized she'd been holding her breath as Commissioner Lopez spoke.

"Watching you and hearing you speak, and seeing all of these folks supporting you, I see no reason you shouldn't be allowed to continue training at the school. I also see no reason to revoke Victory Academy's license."

Corto finally raised his head. MJ stared at him, just like everyone else did.

Corto's face looked twisted, as if he were a clay sculpture someone had mashed with their fists.

MJ had never seen such fury and rage in someone's face before.

"Mr. Corto," the commissioner addressed him formally, and with what sounded like very forced patience. "It seems to me that you have a bit of an unhealthy fixation on Mr.

Arellano and his business, but that's a matter we'll address separately. Is that understood?"

Corto didn't say anything else. He walked out of the room again without looking at any of them.

MJ watched him go. She'd never seen anyone in real life look as hateful as he just did, like a villain in a movie.

She thought about the masked man on the roof. It was hard to think of an official-looking adult in a suit and tie like Corto having something to do with such an awful person committing such awful acts, but for whatever reason, Corto hated the school *so much.*

What if Corto had hired that masked man to attack the school, she wondered.

"As far as the matter before us today," Commissioner Lopez concluded, "it's the commission's ruling that there is no evidence of neglect or endangerment, and Victory Academy's license is hereby upheld."

Beside MJ, Tika and the other students and wrestlers began to cheer. MJ's mother even threw her arms around her. MJ couldn't believe how fast her mother had gone from not wanting them to be here and questioning whether MJ should even be allowed to keep going to Victory Academy to being overjoyed that the school would stay open.

The biggest surprise for her, however, was Zina. MJ felt

arms encircling her shoulders from behind, and in the next moment Zina was pressing her cheek against MJ's.

"I'm sorry, I acted like a jerk," Zina whispered, and it sounded like she was on the verge of crying.

It made MJ feel so happy to hear those words that she was ready to start crying, too.

"No, I was a jerk," she said, clutching Zina's arms with her hands. "A lot of the stuff you said was true, I just didn't know how to tell you."

"You were so great!" Zina congratulated her, laughing even as she sniffled and blinked tears away.

MJ just closed her eyes and held on to her friend.

When MJ opened her eyes again, she looked up at Papi, who only smiled a very small, reserved smile.

MJ was starting to understand that for Mr. Arellano, that was as good as jumping around and cheering.

She wanted to join in and celebrate with them. She wanted to feel happy and victorious too. MJ *did* feel relieved, but she couldn't stop thinking about the idea that the masked man was somehow working for Corto, and that thought kept her from really feeling like they'd won.

MJ didn't want to bring everybody else down, and she didn't think it was the time or place to tell Papi about her theory.

So she forced a smile onto her lips and hugged and slapped hands with Tika and the rest of them, pretending to feel things she didn't.

MJ was tired of doing that, but sometimes it felt like you had to, if only to help other people feel better.

BLOW OFF

Mr. Arellano was yelling at Jason Killgore for pouring cerveza over the steaks as they cooked on the grill.

After the hearing, everyone from Victory Academy who'd attended went to the school to celebrate. MJ's mother had taken the afternoon off but had to return to work to make up the time she missed. Mr. Arellano promised to take MJ home after the party, and her mother agreed to let her join the last-minute celebration.

When they arrived back at Victory Academy, Mr. Arellano lifted the big loading door of the warehouse and set up a barbecue grill right on the sidewalk outside. He'd stopped off at a carnicería on the way, and soon carne asada was sizzling and smoking in the open air of the city.

"We got kids here who are going to eat that!" Papi yelled at the wrestler who he'd left to work the grill, snatching the bottle of beer from the younger man's hand.

"It'll cook off!" Killgore protested. "It's just for flavor! It puts hair on their chest."

"I'll pull the hairs out of your chest, braid them together, and stuff them up your nose, jabroni."

"You know I'm waxed smooth as a baby, Papi," Killgore teased him while rubbing his chest through his T-shirt.

Mr. Arellano just shook his head and drank the rest of Killgore's beer.

The older students and pros were gathered, Tika in the middle of them, along the apron of one of the training rings, drinking beers of their own and laughing.

MJ, Zina, and the other younger students of Victory Academy huddled together in their own group near the vending machines, holding sodas and sports drinks and trying to act like the adults.

Mr. Arellano finished the cerveza and went back to the task of wrapping hot dogs in strips of raw bacon, preparing them for the grill top.

"If you never been across the border," he announced, "*this* is how they do it outside lucha arenas in Mexico. And when you have one of these it will change your life! ¡Créanme!"

"Cuentanos más, Papi!" Tika teased the old man.

"You just wait," Mr. Arellano said as he began laying the bacon-wrapped hot dogs across the blackened bars of the grill.

MJ downed the rest of her sports drink. She wasn't really thirsty, despite how hot it was in the school, even with the giant door open. She couldn't think of anything interesting to say to the other kids, and drinking gave her something to do, and it distracted her from worrying about not being able to think of anything interesting to say.

Thankfully, Zina didn't seem to have that problem.

"You did good today," she told MJ. "Real good. You really earned your spot."

It meant a lot to MJ, hearing Zina say that, but it also made MJ feel guilty about the fight they'd had.

"You deserve to be on the shows more than I do," MJ admitted.

Zina shrugged. "I'll get there. And since you're all famous now you can put me over when I do, and it'll make me look good."

"Put you over?" MJ asked, confused.

Zina laughed and shook her head. "You can let me win," she explained. "God, girl, you do still have a lot to learn."

MJ knew Zina wasn't making fun of her, and MJ didn't

take it that way. It was true, *she* did have a lot to learn, and she was excited about learning all of it.

Zina finished her soda and crushed the can in her hand. The nearest trash can was several yards away, beside the last vending machine in the row. Zina lined up the shot and released the can like a basketball. It sailed smoothly into the trash can, falling right through the middle.

MJ tried the same thing with the empty plastic bottle in her hand, but when she tossed it the bottle hit the rim of the trash can and bounced to the floor.

"I suck," MJ said.

"We'll work on that too," Zina assured her.

It was weird to her, how there'd been so much tension and anger between her and Zina, and now they were like best friends. MJ had never been through that with another girl before. She supposed it was like how families can argue and fight and then go back to being there for each other. That thought made MJ smile, the idea that she was forming that kind of relationship with Zina.

Zina got up to retrieve MJ's bottle and dunk it into the trash can. She stuck her tongue out and made a silly face as she did, and MJ started laughing. It was so ridiculous she had to look away to get herself to stop.

That's when she saw it. Her breath caught in her throat, and her eyes grew wide and filled with shock and fear. It was little more than a shape in the dark, but through the corner of one of the warehouse windows, she saw the mask. It was the green eagle from the rooftop, the luchador's máscara worn by the man who threw that box of rats at MJ and almost caused her to fall to her death.

Then she blinked, and the masked face was gone.

It happened so fast that MJ wasn't sure it had ever really been there in the first place. She'd had a long, emotional day. Her head had felt like a spinning top more than a few times during the last several hours. She could very easily have been imagining things.

It felt real, though. It felt too real, even.

Zina's hand falling gently on MJ's shoulder snapped her out of it.

"Are you okay?" MJ's friend asked.

"Uh, yeah. I'm good."

She wanted to tell Zina about the vision she'd just had, but something held MJ back. Maybe it was her uncertainty about what she had or hadn't just seen. Maybe she didn't want to ruin the joyful mood they were all sharing in that moment.

"¡Miren! We're ready to go here!" Mr. Arellano announced. "But before you all start stuffing your faces, I want to say something."

All the conversation faded to silence as the students and

wrestlers turned their attention to Papi.

MJ didn't know what he was going to say. She was still distracted. The smell of the grilled bacon and carne asada was also making her mouth fill with water and her stomach rumble.

"I'm an old man," Mr. Arellano began.

"We know," Tika quickly agreed, and everyone around her laughed.

"What I'm saying is," Papi went on, giving Tika a hard glance, "I've seen a lot. I've been through a lot. And today wasn't the first time they tried to shut me down. Every Chicano business owner I know has danced with the city. But I have to tell y'all the truth, today was the first time I was really worried this place might have to close."

The silence felt heavier after he said that. No one made any jokes. It was rare for them all to hear Papi admit to something like that. He was always their source of strength.

"But it won't," he reminded them all, and his voice sounded lighter and happier. "We are still here, and we are not going anywhere. I mostly just want to thank all of you for showing up today to stand by the school. You showed me your heart, and I'm proud of all of you. I also want to thank the newest member of our familia, Maya, for stepping up. She may be small, but she showed me her heart the first time she turned up at my door and wouldn't take no for an answer. And she showed even more heart today."

"To MJ!" Tika toasted, jubilantly.

Everyone yelled, "To MJ!"

They all looked at her as they did. She wasn't ready for that, for any of it. Her body felt hot and she wanted to look at the floor, but MJ didn't. She didn't want to hide in that moment. It felt good to be seen by them all, and to know they were proud of her. She saw smiles on their faces, and she smiled back.

Mr. Arellano raised his bottle.

"La Raza!" he toasted.

"La Raza!" they all answered back in one voice.

"Victoria!" Papi added, saluting the school by calling out the Spanish word for "victory."

Again, they all repeated the toast loudly and with feeling, and then everyone cheered as if they were the crowd at one of the school's Saturday shows.

MJ didn't cheer, not out loud, but inside of her the heart Mr. Arellano had spoken so well of a moment ago was practically singing.

GRUDGE MATCH

Mr. Arellano dropped MJ off at her house after the party. It was late, but her mother wouldn't be home for a while yet. MJ assured Papi that it was okay, and that she often let herself into the house and looked after herself until her mother got home.

"Did you have fun?" he asked her.

"Yeah, I did. Lots. Thank you, Papi. Everyone was super nice."

"I think you deserved to be the guest of honor."

Hearing that made MJ feel good, but it also embarrassed her.

"I just told the truth, Papi," she said. "That's all."

"You did more than that," he assured her.

As much as she loved hearing him praise her, that one thought from the hearing was still tugging at the squishy parts of her brain.

"Papi?"

"Something on your mind?"

"Do you think . . . Mr. Corto . . . could he have something to do with whoever I saw on the roof of the school? Like, maybe he paid that guy to mess with us?"

Mr. Arellano actually laughed.

"Corto doesn't have the cojones for something so diabolical. He's a bureaucrat."

"A what?"

"He's a little man with a stupid clipboard and no real power. He's only dangerous if there's a form he can fill out with a pencil."

"But he hates us so much! He hates you!"

"He hates *wrestling*. I'm sure he gives other schools just as much trouble as us. He wouldn't go that far just to close one down. He wouldn't take the risk. He's a coward. I bet he's never gotten his hands dirty his whole life. He tried to shut us down his way, the pencil-pusher way. And he lost. He's got no teeth now. You took them away. He can't hurt us anymore."

It made sense, if what Papi said was true. If Corto had anything to do with the masked man, he could go to jail for it. Why would anyone risk that just because they didn't like wrestling?

"It's over, mija," Papi said when he saw the wheels in her head still turning. "Don't worry about it. You did good. And listen, I want to tell you something else."

The old man was quiet for a moment as he stared out through the windshield of his truck, and MJ could tell he was thinking about something.

"What is it?" she asked.

When he looked back at MJ, the expression on his face was another one she hadn't seen him wear before. He looked somehow sad and happy at the same time.

"I wanted to say I'm sorry if I've been hard on you, or made you feel like you disappointed me."

MJ frowned. "No, Papi. You're just trying to teach me. I know that."

He nodded thoughtfully. "That's true, but there's a difference between teaching someone to be tough and being tough on them. Do you understand?"

"I think so."

"I just want you to know that I'm glad you wouldn't take no for an answer about training at the school. I'm proud to be your trainer. You're a good kid, and if you stick with it, you're going to be a great worker."

MJ didn't know what to say. She felt a pleasant swelling

in her chest and warmth spread through her body. It was a good feeling, and one she wanted to hold onto.

"Thank you, Papi."

He seemed satisfied with that, and he smiled at her.

"I have to go run some errands, and I'll see you at the school, okay?"

MJ nodded. "Okay."

"Buenas noches, Chica Relámpaga."

Mr. Arellano had never called MJ by her Lightning-Girl ring name before. He'd allowed it to be bestowed on her, just as he'd allowed her to wear his grandson's mask, but MJ realized this was the first time the old man had called her by that name.

It was one of the best feelings ever.

She climbed down from the truck, replaying in her mind the words he'd just spoken to her. She waved goodbye to the old man as he drove away.

MJ went inside and got a soda from the refrigerator, even though she wasn't really thirsty. She wasn't sure what to do now. She should've felt great. MJ had helped save the school. Papi's words were precisely what she'd wanted to hear since she started training at Victory Academy.

Something didn't feel right to her, though.

MJ went to her bedroom and set the soda down, unopened. She didn't feel like sitting or lying down. She didn't feel like watching anything on TV or her tablet.

What was it that was *bugging* her so much?

She remembered Corto's face as the commission gave their decision. She also couldn't stop thinking about the masked man outside Victory Academy with the box full of rats. She couldn't stop thinking about how much hate Corto clearly had in his heart for them, and how Papi assured her it was just a hatred of wrestling.

MJ couldn't accept that. She wanted to know why he hated them so much. She had only been as angry as Corto about one thing in her whole life, and she knew exactly what the reason was. MJ couldn't imagine Corto felt rage like that unless something horrible was at the center of it, just as the most horrible thing that had ever happened to her was at the center of her rage.

MJ opened the internet browser on her phone and typed "Neal Corto" into Google. The search didn't return anything surprising. It brought up links to the State Athletic Commission's website, and there was a picture of the man with a short paragraph about him. There was also a link to Corto's LinkedIn profile. Neither page told her much: just where he went to school and that his hobbies included golf and poker. All the pictures of him were recent and showed him in his suit with a big smile on his face that almost made him look like a nice guy.

MJ knew better.

He didn't seem to be on Facebook or Twitter or any other social networking website. She frowned, not sure what else to do, or even what she was looking for by searching his name.

She thought about the hooded man again. MJ highlighted Corto's name and deleted it. She typed "lucha green eagle" into the browser and performed a search. She scrolled through drawings posted on art websites and crafts for sale through places like Etsy. Finally, she started to see references to wrestlers, a lot of them recent, but none of them wearing the mask she'd seen.

Another thought occurred to her, and she modified the search by adding Papi's name—not his real name, but El Hacha Rojo, his lucha name.

After hitting "search" and scrolling past several unrelated links, MJ found what she hadn't even known she was looking for.

It was a scan of an old pro-wrestling newsletter called *Heat Seeker* that was printed on paper. MJ had read about these on Wikipedia. Before everything was on the internet, there were things called "dirt sheets" that reported on the behind-the-scenes news of the wrestling business. This must've been one of them.

The date on the scanned issue of *Heat Seeker* read,

"June 1998." That was the month and year it was published. There were several different stories on the page she was looking at, but the biggest one with the largest headline read, "Backstage Lucha Brawl!" It had two pictures side by side. One was of a man in a red mask with an axe blade over the eyes, and the other picture was of a man in a black hood with an eagle, exactly like the one MJ had seen.

The story itself was about a luchador called Green Eagle who got into a fight backstage at a wrestling show with El Hacho Rojo II. MJ realized the wrestler Green Eagle fought wasn't Mr. Arellano, but his son, who had taken on the same name and mask.

She read the story. The fight wasn't part of a wrestling match or a storyline. This was a real fight that wasn't supposed to happen. Apparently Green Eagle accused El Hacho Rojo II and his father of conspiring to take Green Eagle's spot on the card. The story went on to say that Green Eagle was fired from the wrestling company for starting the fight, and that his wrestling license had since been taken away.

There was another picture at the bottom of the article that was taken during the fight. MJ recognized Mr. Arellano standing in the background, even though he was twenty years younger. He was watching what was happening with a shocked and angry look on his face. The picture actually showed Green Eagle without his mask on. It was grainy and old, but his face was clear enough, and MJ thought she recognized it too.

She opened another tab and searched Neal Corto's name again. She opened the State Athletic Commission page with his picture on it and zoomed in on his face. Then she switched back to the image from the newsletter. She went back and forth between the two pictures several times before she was certain.

Corto hadn't hired the masked man.

Corto *was* the masked man.

He was Green Eagle. He used to be a luchador, and it all must have ended for him after that backstage fight. That was why he was so mad at them. He blamed Papi's family for ruining his career.

Neal Corto didn't hate wrestling, he *loved* wrestling, and losing it made him hate everyone who still had it in their lives, especially those he blamed for taking it away from him.

Losing what you loved most in life could make you feel and do things you never imagined. MJ understood that to be true.

She couldn't be sure if Corto became a member of the athletic commission in order to get back at Papi for derailing his career as Green Eagle, or if he found out about

Victory Academy after taking the job and decided to use his position to get revenge.

Either way, it was clear Corto had become obsessed with ruining the old man and taking down the school, and if that was true then MJ believed Corto wouldn't stop just because the commission hadn't ruled the way he wanted.

And at that moment no one except him and MJ knew how much danger Victory Academy was still in.

* * * * * * * * * *

BURNING DOWN THE HOUSE

MJ couldn't reach anyone.

She wanted to scream in frustration. Her mother was working late, and she had the bad habit of not charging her phone during the day so that it was dead if she stayed at the office past five o'clock. When MJ called her mother's work directly, an automated voice message answered her instead of the receptionist who took calls during business hours, and the machine voice just told her to leave a message and someone would get back to her the next day.

Victory Academy didn't have a landline. Mr. Arellano wasn't home next door, and he wasn't answering his phone either.

MJ left a voicemail message: "Papi, it's Maya. I have

something I have to tell you. You *have* to call me back. The school is still in trouble."

She tried Tika next, and when no one answered she didn't even bother leaving a voicemail.

MJ paced back and forth across the floor of her bedroom, not knowing what else to do.

MJ looked over at her windowsill. The drone she'd crashed into Mr. Arellano's backyard was sitting on it. It was still broken. She'd had plenty of time to get it fixed since then, but she hadn't thought about it. She hadn't needed to. MJ was no longer the sad girl who sat alone at her window after school every day dive-bombing empty soda cans with her toy. She had somewhere to go and something to do. She had somewhere she belonged.

That place was Victory Academy, and MJ wasn't going to let anything happen to it.

The year before, her mother had installed the Lyft app on MJ's phone. She'd made it clear it was for emergencies only, no exceptions. MJ didn't know if her mother would think this situation counted as an emergency, but if not, then MJ was ready to accept the consequences.

She ordered the Lyft with trembling fingertips, and then put on her boots and her jacket before heading outside to wait in front of the house. Part of her was afraid her mother would return home at that moment and find out what she was doing, and another part of MJ hoped her mother would show up so she could just cancel the Lyft and explain to her mother what was happening.

A few minutes later the car she ordered pulled up, and neither Papi nor her mother were anywhere in sight. MJ hesitated before climbing inside. The driver was an older man who seemed nice enough. He asked her if she needed a charger for her phone, and MJ told him she didn't. Fortunately, that was the only question he asked her.

She thought about calling Papi again, but instead, perhaps because MJ didn't want the driver to hear her ranting into her phone, she sent Mr. Arellano a quick text message. She kept it short, letting him know she was headed back to the school, and that he needed to meet her there as soon as possible because it was an emergency.

MJ felt like she was bouncing in her seat the whole ride over, she felt so anxious. She didn't know why. There was just something inside of her that said if she waited for tomorrow to tell Papi what she'd learned, it would be too late.

When they arrived, MJ found she was scared to get out of the car. It was hours past dark, and she'd never been here this late without Papi or her mother accompanying her.

"Are you sure this is the right place?" the driver asked her.

MJ nodded quickly. "My grandfather is waiting for me. It's okay."

She felt bad lying, maybe because the driver seemed so friendly and his concern sounded genuine.

She climbed out of the car and waited for him to pull away. There were no lights on inside Victory Academy that MJ could see from outside. There were no cars parked in front of it this late, either.

Despite how it looked, MJ was surprised to find that not only was the front door unlocked, but also open, just a crack. MJ gently pushed it open wider until she could slip inside.

"Papi!" MJ called out as she walked into the school. "Are you here?"

No one answered her, yet somehow MJ knew she wasn't alone. The warehouse was as dark as it had looked from the outside. MJ tasted acid in the back of her throat. She couldn't remember the last time she'd felt so afraid. Despite that, she wasn't about to run away.

MJ felt her way across the concrete blocks of the wall until her fingertips touched cool metal. She knew it was the power box that worked the ring lights. Her hand closed around the rubber grip that covered the handle, and she flipped it to the on position.

The center of the warehouse and the show ring set up there were suddenly bathed in light. The ring wasn't empty, either. There was a lone figure casting a stubby shadow from the middle of the canvas.

It was the man in the black and green eagle mask, the one who unleashed the rats. He was wearing gloves and a long leathery trench coat. A steel chair from the stacks that were usually piled against the wall was unfolded and sitting beside him.

In one of those gloved hands he was holding onto what looked like a can of gasoline.

He didn't move and he didn't speak. He just stared across the warehouse at MJ through the shadow-filled eyeholes of his máscara.

"I know it's you," she said, trying to keep her voice from shaking, trying to sound tough. "I know why you're doing this. I know you blame Papi for ruining your career."

He reached up with his empty hand and slowly peeled back that lucha hood.

Corto smiled at her. His eyes, now that she could make them out, were filled with anger.

"Papi," he spat, as if the name were a curse word. "He's not your father, you know. He acts like it, but he doesn't care about any of you. You're just money to him, and a way for him to still feel important, like he matters. Even though he stopped mattering in this business a long time ago."

"He mattered more than you!" MJ shot back, her own anger surprising her.

Corto's warped smile faded, twisting into a sneer.

"You don't know anything about it! I had more talent in my finger than he or any of his nieces or nephews had in their whole bodies! But all he cared about was giving his family every good spot on the card, every opportunity that should've been mine!"

MJ reached inside her jacket and pulled out her phone.

"I don't care what you think he did to you. It doesn't give you the right to attack the school! I'm calling the police!"

Corto reached inside his trench coat pocket, as well. He didn't pull out a phone, though. He pulled out a cigarette lighter.

"Don't do it," he warned her, holding up the lighter and sparking a flame.

MJ paused, holding the phone in front of her. She looked above and behind Corto.

For the first time, she noticed long, thin black cords hanging down from the lights above the rings. Those cords had never been there before. They ran up into the rafters, and several strands snaked down the walls. She could see those had been fed into electrical outlets throughout the school.

MJ looked back at the gas can Corto was holding, and her eyes widened in shock as she realized those cords were fuses. He must have been using that steel chair to help hang them.

He was planning to light them on fire and burn down Victory Academy.

"That's right," Corto said, seeing the look on her face. "This place will be crumbling ash before anyone you call can get here. I promise you that."

MJ didn't want to believe he meant it, but she could see that he did.

"What ... what do you want?"

"I want you to bring that phone to me, *now*!"

She didn't know what else to do. Her legs didn't seem to want to carry her forward, but she made them, stepping across the cement floor with her arm extended out, as if the phone in her hand was leading her. She walked it next to the ring and held it toward the ropes.

"In the ring," Corto ordered her. "Put the phone on the mat right in front of me."

MJ never took her eyes off him. She climbed up onto the apron and under the bottom rope, standing up slowly and shakily.

"That's right," Corto said. "Bring it here."

MJ's heart was pounding so hard she could hear it

between her ears. She took two steps across the canvas and knelt, slowly, lowering her arm to place the phone on the mat. The whole time she was staring at the sparked lighter he still held in his gloved hand. She didn't know what he would do after she gave up her phone, but MJ had to believe he wasn't going to stop.

Moving as fast as she could, MJ popped up and threw her phone like a pitcher hurling a baseball. It hit Corto's glove and knocked the lighter from his hand, extinguishing the flame. As soon as she released the phone, MJ was leaping forward to grab hold of the gas can. Her only thought was to snatch it from him and run away.

MJ hugged her arms around the can and turned to bolt, hoping to rip it from his grip as she did. Corto was much stronger than her, though. It was like trying to pull a tree stump out of the ground. MJ lost her footing and stumbled. At the same time, Corto swung his arm, sending her flying backward. As she did, the metal body of the gas can hit her head. Everything went black for just a second, and the next thing MJ knew her body was crashing against the ropes.

She didn't hit them the way Tika had trained her to, and they bit her painfully all over her body. Instead of gliding gracefully back across the ring, it felt as though MJ was being thrown down to the mat by strong, wiry arms. She didn't break a clean bump, either. MJ landed hard on her hip and shoulder, and the muscles in both places screamed angrily at her in protest.

She tried to ignore the pain and the fear and the panic bubbling in her brain. MJ pushed herself to her feet, finding that getting up after taking a hard fall was second nature to her now. She blinked, her vision blurry from the hits she'd just taken. Corto looked like nothing but one big ugly blob to her.

She ran at him again, this time not even aiming for the gas can. MJ didn't know what her plan was at this point, really. She didn't have one. She only knew she had to stop him, someway, somehow.

Fortunately, she didn't have to figure out what to do when she reached him. Unfortunately, the reason she didn't have to figure it out was because Corto scooped her up with the practiced ease of a former wrestler and body-slammed her to the mat, hard, taking no care to protect her the way an opponent would in a real match.

The canvas had never before felt so unforgiving to her as she hit it. All the breath left her body, rushing out through her mouth and nose as roughly as a stampede of horses. She seemed to be able to feel every single bone in her body, and they all hurt.

"You're not a lucha hero," he told her, breathing hard from their short tussle. "You're just a dumb little kid with bad timing. If you're lucky I'll drag you outside so you can watch this place burn."

MJ couldn't look up at him, but she felt his heavy boots stomping away from where she lay. A moment later there was a hollow metal crash somewhere outside the ring, and she realized Corto had tossed his gas can away.

MJ rolled over even though every aching part of her body felt like it was screaming at her to stop moving. Her head was her loudest opponent. All her brain seemed to want her to do was sleep. She blinked, feeling something wet sting her eyes. MJ didn't know whether what was in her eyes was tears or blood, but it hurt. She wiped it away with her hands, blinking more until the world came back into focus.

MJ looked up from the canvas. Corto had climbed the ring ropes and was sitting on the top turnbuckle. In one hand he held the end of one of the fuses he'd hung from the lights. In his other hand was the lighter he'd threatened her with. He must've picked it up from wherever it had fallen.

He was getting ready to spark the fuse.

She opened her mouth to beg him to stop, but no words came out. At first she thought it was because she was afraid, and she wanted to curse herself for being too little and too weak to stop him. There was something else stopping her from crying out, though. There was something inside telling her not to beg and plead. Her brain repeated to her that this was *her* school. It felt more like home to her than that rented house her mother had been forced to move them into. It was everything Mr. Arellano had. This building meant something to him, and to his people, to *their* people.

Seeing Corto perched on the top rope, looking up at him from the ring floor like that, reminded MJ of the final moments in her very first match with Tika. It was a weird thing to think about at a time like this, but it gave her an idea. She wished Tika were there now to help her.

She wasn't, though. No one was going to help her or coach her or hold her hand through this. She had to do it for herself.

MJ pressed her hands against the ring floor and pushed her body up from the mat. Her legs felt like the spaghetti her mother always boiled for far too long, but she stood on them all the same. The top turnbuckle looked higher than it ever had, and Corto was much taller than Tika.

You'll never make it, another voice inside her head promised her.

MJ knew that voice well. It was the same voice that

told her not to go up to other kids and try to make them her friends. It was the same voice that told her to quit gymnastics rather than stand up to her teammates when they treated her badly or excluded her.

That voice didn't belong in Victory Academy. This was the one place that voice had never held her back or stopped her from doing what she wanted.

I know I can't make it, MJ told herself, *but Lightning Girl can do anything.*

She didn't need the mask in that moment.

MJ put one foot in front of her and suddenly she was sprinting across the ring. Her legs seemed to feel stronger with each step she took, and by the time MJ was ready to make the leap the rest of her body felt just as strong.

Corto looked down at her in surprise, holding the sparked lighter just inches from the first fuse.

"Wait—" he started to say.

But MJ was already flying up toward him.

Her feet landed even more firmly on the ropes than they had the first time she'd tried this. MJ quickly bounced off them and jumped up onto Corto's shoulders, locking her legs around his little head with its slicked back hair.

The impact made him drop the lighter outside the ring. He had to wrap his gloved hands around the top rope just to keep from falling off the turnbuckle. The lighter must have landed in some spilt gas from the can, because in the next second MJ heard flames burst and crackle to life somewhere below them. She could feel the heat from the newly born fire on her skin.

There was no time to worry about that, however.

MJ launched the top half of her body backward, tightening her legs around Corto's neck. Instead of flipping the man off the top rope, however, MJ found the back of her head smacking against the middle turnbuckle. She hung upside-down limply, dangling from Corto like she was a necklace. He was still sitting firmly on the top rope.

She could hear him laughing above her. It was an ugly sound, almost like he didn't understand what laughing was, or like he didn't know how to feel the way you're supposed to feel when you laugh.

"That stuff doesn't work in real life, little girl!" he snarled down at her.

MJ was still hanging from his neck by her legs. She leaned her head back, beginning to panic. Then she saw the steel chair. It was folded up and lying flat directly below her. It must've gotten knocked into the corner when she ran at Corto the first time.

MJ could feel Corto's gloved hands closing around her

waist. She didn't know what he was planning to do with her, but MJ knew she wouldn't like it. He stood up on the second rope, holding her tightly as he did.

She reached down at the last second and grabbed the folding chair by its legs.

"I don't want to hurt you, little girl," he told her.

"*Lightning* Girl!" MJ screamed as she clinched her legs tight around his neck and pulled herself up.

She swung her arms as hard as she could, bashing the seat of the metal chair against Corto's face. She hit him so hard that she lost her grip on the chair's legs and it went flying out of her hands, but the damage was already done. Sitting on his shoulders and looking down at his unmasked face once again, MJ saw eyes that looked blank and dazed. His hands slipped weakly from where they'd been holding her waist, and his arms hung loosely behind the top rope.

This time she threw the top of herself backward and pulled with her legs, and Corto's whole body went with her. As they flew through the air, the fire spreading across the cement floor of the school reached the tipped over gas can and it blew up, sounding like the blast from half a dozen shotguns and sending a giant spurt of flame up into the air. MJ watched it helplessly from the corner of her eye, her body tensing as it tumbled through the air.

She unlocked her legs and broke the cleanest front bump she could as she landed on the canvas. She was breathing hard, but she hurt less than she had just moments ago. It must have been the adrenalin running through her body.

MJ knew right away that Corto hadn't broken a clean bump. She could tell just from the sound, less like a solid thud and more like someone dropping a bag full of loose tools. His body must have hit the mat at a bad, awkward angle. When she recovered from the flip and the explosion and turned around to see, Corto was lying on his side with his arms folded over him unnaturally. His legs were a messy tangle, and his head was sloped to one side.

He wasn't moving.

MJ scrambled forward in a panic and crawled over to him. MJ was afraid to touch him, but she hovered directly above Corto carefully. She was terrified in that moment that she might have killed the man.

Fortunately, she could see his chest rising and falling. Corto was still breathing, even if he continued to lie there and not move.

Relieved, MJ sat back on the canvas. She closed her eyes and tried to catch her breath, tried to stop her head from spinning.

Then she smelled the smoke and remembered the fire.

MJ gasped and her eyes snapped open. She got up to her knees and peered between the ropes. The flames had almost reached the ring apron. If that cloth caught fire it would spread quickly, she knew, incinerating the ring and igniting the fuses Corto had hung.

MJ rolled across the canvas and slid back under the bottom rope. She picked up the same chair she'd used to whack Corto where it had landed on the floor. There was a fire extinguisher in a metal case with a glass lid bolted to the wall. MJ turned her head away from it as she swung the chair at the case, shattering the glass.

MJ removed the extinguisher, grunting at how heavy it was and using both arms to dislodge it. She quickly read the directions that were printed on a sticker on its body. She started with the spot where the gas can had exploded, where the concentration of flame was the heaviest, blasting it with spray from the extinguisher. It took a few seconds, and MJ started to worry there was too much, but then the fire started dying.

She followed each trail of flame from there, snuffing them out before they spread from the floor to any of the rings. When she was done it looked like it had snowed inside Victory Academy.

When the last patch of fire had been put out, MJ set

down the extinguisher and looked back at where Corto was still sprawled out on the canvas. He wasn't stirring yet, but she knew he'd wake up eventually. She needed to call the police, but it would also take them a while to get there.

So first MJ ran to where the students' lockers were set up. She opened the one that Corrina used when she trained and worked their shows. Corrina kept extra gear and gimmicks in there. MJ grabbed a pair of the handcuffs that decorated her ring jacket and sprinted back to the ring.

Corto's body was much heavier lying on the canvas than it had felt when she flipped him through the air. MJ could only drag him a few feet, but it was enough to cuff one of his wrists to the bottom rope.

The ringtone of her own phone made MJ jump. She looked over and saw it lighting up on the mat where it had landed after she'd thrown it.

MJ crawled over to the ringing phone and saw the words "Mr. Arellano" on its screen. She picked it up and answered the call.

"Papi?" she said.

"Maya," his voice greeted her, sounding concerned. "What's going on? Is everything okay?"

MJ didn't even know where to begin. She stared across the ring at Corto, battered and handcuffed to the ring.

Then she looked out across the warehouse floor, blackened from the fire and dusted white from the extinguisher.

Despite how frightening and painful and difficult the last few minutes had been, MJ found herself smiling.

"Yeah, sí," she said to him. "Everything is fine."

EPILOGUE: PAPI

It was the first day of summer vacation and her mother and Mr. Arellano brought MJ to finally visit her father's grave.

She was wearing a dress, a black one with a white stripe around the middle that her abuelita had made for her. MJ hated dresses, but both her mother and Mr. Arellano agreed it was appropriate for the occasion. He'd also given her a small bouquet of colorful flowers with ruffled petals that were red, white, and green. Their stems were tied together with a white ribbon.

She kept her mouth closed for almost the entire drive, because when she opened it, MJ found her breathing was loud and shaky. Surprisingly, that painful knot in her stomach wasn't there. Instead she felt little pinprick sensations all up and down her arms and legs. She expected to be sad, even angry, but she didn't know why she felt so anxious about going. MJ knew what was waiting for them. They'd driven here several times before. It wasn't like it was going to be a surprise.

Still, she felt more anxious than she could remember feeling, maybe ever, even all the other times she'd tried to make this trip.

The cemetery was green and beautifully kept, like the park MJ always tried to imagine it was. It didn't look like a depressing place, but it definitely made her feel sad.

Her mother pulled the car over a few minutes after they drove through the cemetery gates. Even though MJ had been here before, on the day of the funeral and the times after that when she couldn't get out of the car, none of it looked familiar to her.

She was staring through the window, thinking about how strange and new it all seemed, when Mr. Arellano opened the door for her. He smiled down at MJ softly. He was wearing the same suit he'd had on the day they first met, and he'd yelled at her in his backyard. Thinking about it actually made MJ feel a little better, but it only lasted until she got out of the car.

She could see it, the headstone; and MJ suddenly

remembered exactly where she was and how it had looked on that day, the day they buried her father. The memory didn't make her sadder, oddly, but it did make her even more nervous for some reason.

"Do you want us to go with you?" her mother asked, smiling even though her eyes were sad.

"I'm okay," MJ assured them.

She wasn't sure that was true.

They let her walk across the grass alone. Her father's grave was marked with a big, shiny marble stone that had his name, Victor Gabriel Medina, chiseled on it, along with the date he was born and the date he died, more than a year ago now. Below that, a picture of Saint Faustina was painted on the marble. She had a kind face and soft eyes that looked down, as if she was watching over Victor.

Underneath the image of the saint, there was a quote, something Faustina had said before she passed away and was made a saint: "Love endures everything, love is stronger than death, love fears nothing."

MJ knelt in the grass in front of the stone, her fists closed tight around the bound stems of the flowers.

"I'm sorry," she said, because that seemed like the right thing to say, and nothing else came to her in that moment.

Then MJ really thought about the words she'd just spoken, and the words of Saint Faustina, and she realized she *was* sorry. Suddenly, she was filled with guilt. This was such a lonely place, and he'd been stuck here without his family this whole time because she'd been angry and selfish and afraid to come here. She hadn't thought at all about him being alone. She'd just been so mad, not even about her father dying, but about him *leaving* them, as if it were a choice he'd made. She knew how wrong that was now.

She read Saint Faustina's quote again.

MJ started to cry.

"I'm so sorry, Papi," she said again, the words drowning in the tears that poured down her face.

It had happened so suddenly. Her father hadn't been sick, not at all. They thought he was perfectly healthy. He played baseball for his company team every year. He went to the gym several times a week. He ran marathons to help raise money for their church.

Then one day he'd dropped dead, with no warning. His heart just stopped beating.

It wasn't fair and it didn't make any sense. It took so long for MJ to even be able to understand and accept that it had happened, and then all she could feel was anger.

"You were my only friend," she whispered, reaching out a trembling hand to touch the headstone.

It felt so cold, and that only made MJ cry harder.

"You were the only friend I had. Mom tries, and I love

her, but you were always the one—"

She couldn't finish, and she didn't need to. Her father knew how close they were, and how much MJ needed him, needed someone who understood her and liked the things she liked and encouraged her to do the things she wanted to do. He loved being that for her. He devoted so much of his time to her. She knew he never would have left them if he had a choice.

MJ wasn't angry anymore, but all that anger was replaced by something worse in that moment, the grief she hadn't wanted to deal with. Being mad was always easier for her than feeling sad, and without holding onto that anger MJ suddenly couldn't feel anything except that sadness.

She cried without trying to speak again for a long time, like letting a fire burn itself out. There was nothing else she could do, and a part of her knew she needed this, needed to let it all out.

It felt like being sick and throwing up. It was awful while it was happening, but when it was finally over you felt better, even if you were still sick. You felt lighter and freer, like you could finally rest and start healing.

MJ took a deep breath, and then another.

By her fifth deep breath she felt well enough to speak again.

"I have some new friends now," she said, louder and with less hurt in her voice. "It's not the same. Nothing could be the same. But it's . . . better? It's a little better, I guess. I just wish you could come and watch me, the things I'm doing. You'd love it so much. It's just like we used to watch on TV. I mean, I'm not good like that, not yet, but still. I will be some day. You'll see. At least I hope you'll see, in some way."

Thinking about wrestling helped, and about all the people at Victory Academy: Tika and Zina and Creepshow and Corrina. She thought about how it was almost like the horrible fight she'd had with Zina never happened, and how weird and amazing a thing that was. She'd never had a friend like Zina before, let alone had to figure out how to fix that kind of friendship after it took such a hard hit. MJ felt like the two of them were actually closer now because of it, and that was even more amazing to her.

She thought about all of that and nodded as if she were trying to tell herself that it was okay, or at least that it was going to be okay.

For the first time, she was glad she'd finally decided to come here.

"I'm going to Mexico with Mom and Mr. Arellano this summer. We're going to visit his son and his grandson, like I'm visiting you now. It'll be sad, but I'm excited, too. Mr.

Arellano is going to take us to see the real lucha; at least that's what he says. Mom and I are going to see some of the family, too. Abuelita and the others. Mom says we're going to do that more. I think that was the hard thing for her, you know? Seeing Abuelita and Tío Kevin and all of them from your side. It made her sad. But I think we're both ready to start doing the things that make us sad again, so they get easier."

MJ swallowed, hard.

"Everyone calls Mr. Arellano 'Papi,' you know, because he's kind of a dad to all of us at the school. I call him that too sometimes. I just want you to know, though . . . it's not the same. It won't ever be the same. I'm really lucky to have him, but I'll always miss you. You'll always be my papi. Always."

She laid the flowers in her hands down gently on the grass in front of the headstone.

"I promise from now on I'll come visit you every weekend when we're home. I love you, Papi."

MJ kissed the palm of her hand and pressed it against the marble. It didn't feel as cold the second time. She felt like she might start crying again, so she took her hand away and stood up, sucking back her wet breath.

Standing up quickly like that started her thinking about something. She thought about everything that had happened in the past few months. She thought about bump training. She thought about Corto and how he'd let his sadness and anger turn him into a monster. She thought about the fight they'd had in the ring when he tried to burn Victory Academy to the ground.

MJ realized that the answer to every hard thing she'd faced over the past year was getting back up again after you'd been knocked down. If you stayed down, that's when all those bad feelings took control of you, and that's when you lost. Corto had stayed down after his wrestling career ended. He'd stopped fighting for what he wanted and started hating and blaming everyone else instead.

You had to get back up. You always had to get back up, no matter how hard it was.

MJ looked over and saw her mother and Mr. Arellano waiting patiently for her by the car, watching her with warm smiles, ready to do or give her whatever she needed to help her through this. Seeing them there like that made her think about something else.

It was a lot easier to get back up when you had help.

* * * * * * * * * *

ACKNOWLEDGMENTS

This book wouldn't have been written without my agent, DongWon Song, who encouraged me to tell more personal stories and guided me toward finding my voice for middle grade fiction. Greg van Eekhout's work and consultation also helped me greatly in figuring out how I wanted to write books for kids. My wife, Nikki, lent her experiences and perspective to this novel, as she does with all my work, and she remains my most invaluable collaborator. My editor, Ben Rosenthal, has been a constant source of guidance, understanding, and enthusiasm, and I am deeply grateful this book found its publishing champion in him. Carlos Hernandez provided encouragement and valuable insight. Mark Oshiro went out of their way to support this book and me. My mother, Barbara, is always my work's biggest and loudest advocate. This novel is dedicated to my nieces and nephew, but I also want to acknowledge their parents and the rest of my family: Kevin and Katie, Ken and Melissa, and Samantha and Nick. My late father-in-law, Mitch, and my mother-in-law, Jodie, were also integral in bringing the story of *Bump* to life. My master of webs, Jack Townsend, keeps my online presence presentable and up-to-date. Kat Fajardo is a brilliant artist, and her cover illustration captured everything *Bump* is, complimented beautifully by Lisa Vega's design. I, like all authors, am eternally indebted to my copyeditors, Mary Auxier and Laura Harshberger, as well as Tanu Srivastava, Emily Zhu and Vaishali Nayak in marketing, my publicist, Lauren Levite, and of course, the legendary Katherine Tegen herself.

Although Victory Academy is an invention, many of the stories that occur within its walls are taken from my experiences attending the LIWF Doghouse pro wrestling school in Queens, New York, as a kid myself. I owe so much of who I am now to the owner of the Doghouse and LIWF founder, Bobby Lombardi, who was taken from us too soon, and the school's head trainer, Laython Wilkerson, as well as the rest of the Doghouse crew: Dee Erazo, Brandon Silvestry, Dimitrios "Papadon" Papadoniou, Marcello H. Carnevali, Louie Ramos, Jerry Todisco, Bill Pierce, Steve Mack, Angelo Bell, Ed Toscano, John Shea, and many others throughout the years who've come and gone. They were and remain my second family. I'm also grateful to the luchadores I was privileged to work closely with and learn from over my years in the wrestling business, including El Latino/Lemus I, Chavo Guerrero, Sr., and Super Aguilar.

My love of lucha was rekindled by the work and friendship of Keith Rainville, Rafael Navarro, and Christa Faust. They all inspired this book as much as anyone else. Finally, Gino Carusso, the man who "discovered" me and first brought me to the Doghouse to train and always remained invested in my progress and career.